REA

Fict
Foley, Sylvia.
Life in the air ocean

6-8-99

Life in the Air Ocean

Life in the Air Ocean

STORIES BY

SYLVIA FOLEY

Alfred A. Knopf NEW YORK 1999

THIS IS A BORZOI BOOK
PUBLISHED BY ALFRED A. KNOPF, INC.

Copyright © 1999 by Sylvia Foley
All rights reserved under International and Pan-American
Copyright Conventions. Published in the United States by
Alfred A. Knopf, Inc., New York, and simultaneously in
Canada by Random House of Canada Limited, Toronto.
Distributed by Random House, Inc., New York.

www.randomhouse.com

"Life in the Air Ocean" was originally published in *GQ*,
"Cloudland" in *The Antioch Review*, and "Dogfight" in
Open City, in slightly different form.

Library of Congress Cataloging-in-Publication Data
Foley, Sylvia.
Life in the air ocean : stories / by Sylvia Foley. — 1st ed.
p. cm.
ISBN 0-375-40063-X
1. Tennessee—Social life and customs—Fiction.
2. Americans—Colombia—Bogotá—Fiction.
3. Family—Tennessee—Fiction.
I. Title.
PS3556.039177L54   1999   98-14212
813'.54—dc21   CIP

Manufactured in the United States of America
First Edition

For Joyce

ACKNOWLEDGMENTS

I am deeply grateful for my early teachers, in particular Arlene Voelz, Lotte Murphy, Joseph Cichello, Sherrill Aberg, and Kathleen Collins; for Kaylie Jones at The Writer's Voice; and for the faculty and students at Columbia University's School of the Arts, especially Maureen Howard and Joyce Johnson. My heartfelt thanks as well to my agent, Irene Skolnick, and my editor, Victoria Wilson. The Cummington Community of the Arts, the Jewish Foundation for Education of Women, and the family of Leigh Titus provided time and generous support. I am very grateful to each of them.

Warmest thanks to Laura Wetzler for her spirited belief in me; to sensei Annie Ellman and Brooklyn Women's Martial Arts; and to Bethany Becks, Shelley Brenner, Liz Egloff, Suzanne Fox, Vivienne Freund, Amelia Ross, and Nancy Soyer for their friendship. Thanks to my mother and father for their made-up languages; to Dora; and to my sister Mo. Thanks to my companions, sweet Gus and Lila. Always, my love and thanks to Joyce Vinson, who sees me through.

CONTENTS

Life in the Air Ocean

Cave Fish

At the Bloodmobile babies were screaming. Daniel Mowry felt that sinking feeling coming on again. He thought, Like to yowl myself, although his test was over and done with. Dazed, he sat down on a folding chair as the wails of the infants broke over him. He steadied his briefcase against his knee and drank the cup of sugary lemonade the nurse gave him, knowing that within minutes she would make him leave. He told himself his blood was as high octane as the next man's. Then, left hand shaking a little, he peeled back the Band-Aid and examined the stuck pulp of his finger.

He had tried to donate blood and was denied! Here he was at the Carville Red Cross station with the Negro nurse pricking his middle finger, telling him no, and he just didn't get it. His blood had been plenty good enough three, four years ago for the doughfoots over in Korea. He belonged to the U.S. Army then— he wanted to fly, but his eyes were bad. The army took him anyway, once they saw he was smart enough for the SEDs, the Special Engineering Detachment. He spent the war testing rockets in the heat of the New Mexican desert; he could rattle off the flash points of red fuming nitric acid and gasoline, the degrees Fahrenheit a Nike's aluminum skin could withstand. The time-delay squib, that was his idea: take advantage of deceleration, let things cool a bit before firing up the second stage. After his discharge, what was he meant to do with his life? This was him now—a design engineer, an expert in home appliances. Not what he'd dreamed. He tried to tell himself he was making the world safer for women and children, but Iris and the baby hardly seemed to need him that way.

He wasn't a coward. Just now, he had watched the needle rowel his flesh, his own blood well and leak out of him. When the nurse touched the slide to his bleeding finger, he closed his eyes and imagined the rest, how blood coated the clamped glass and was flattened to a single-cell layer under the microscope for her edification. His blood was no good. "Your count's too low," the nurse was telling him, and she knew, somehow, not to look at him as she said it. "You get your wife to cook you up a liver steak tonight." But all he knew was his blood was no good, and there wasn't any liver steak, just eggs, because his wife was sick or something. Lately Iris couldn't stand the sight of raw meat. At home his baby might be screaming; maybe Iris would cradle it and coo to it at the kitchen table. He knew he would go down under the house as soon as he could get away. He was digging himself a real cellar, tunneling down from the crawl space below the kitchen floor. Unheard of in Carville, Tennessee; *What y'all need a hole in the ground for?* people said. Even the guy at the hardware store said it, eyeing him as though Daniel was the one touched in the head.

Waiting for the bus to take him back across town, all Daniel could think about was failure. The dark-reddish nurse in the little room, the smell of the alcohol swabs and the cold test tubes full of jelly blood, blood so thick and black it might have come from horses. She told him to eat iron. He thought of chewing metal: pieces of copper wire, drill scraps, the iron filings he kept in a vial in his toolbox. When the baby was older he planned on showing her how precisely iron followed a magnet, the inert bits quivering as if touched to life. He could make them race across a mirror. He had a predilection for velocity. Friction is the real enemy, he used to announce like a Dick Tracy scientist, smiling at his own joke, but his superiors in the desert had not seen it as such.

The sun was going down. He felt faint and unknotted his tie. Iris would be wanting him home soon for supper. As he boarded the bus he felt something flap at his knee. It was an unfurled umbrella, belonging to the guy nudging him from behind. "C'mon, move it." The guy was wearing a tight blue suit with little Memphis Air wings on the lapel—a pilot, for the love of God. Daniel squeezed his teeth together and gripped the rail. The driver glanced down at him as if he were any shady character, and it was all Daniel could do not to turn around and belt the guy. He took his seat, thinking, Should've given him a good poke in the chest at least, told him, *Watch who you're pushing!* Only he was no fighter. The flyboy would've decked him, maybe cracked his head open on the bus's metal step, and then where would he be. Hell, he might try *not* to die out here on the Carville run; if something were to happen, he couldn't count on his blood working right. Besides, Iris was waiting for him. Those eggs were probably already cooked into rubber in the green kitchen. He pictured her leaning over the ironing board with her long blue-black hair falling across the pad, testing spit on the iron, and he knew he had to get there. He had to get there so he could cook the eggs first the way she liked, a little

runny, with pepper and cheese, and afterward he'd rest
one hand on her neck while he clipped the singed ends
of her hair and she murmured to him about what the
baby was doing now.

A week ago, he had come home to find Iris holding her hand over the baby's mouth, her eyes fixed on
the stove clock. When he asked what was going on,
she took her hand away. "I'm timing the baby," Iris
said. "See the blue lips? She can hold her breath.
Maybe she'll be aquatic." They should put a goldfish
pond in the yard, like the one the Achesons had, laid
to instructions ordered from a magazine. This was
Iris's plan. The kid was all right, of course.

And yesterday the baby had rolled over by itself.
All day Iris had watched it try and finally it had done it.
After supper they went and got the baby and sat out
on the back steps. "See her?" Iris said, laying the baby
on its round belly on the driveway, on a layer of raked
sand. Together they sat and watched while the kid
hunched its shoulders and kicked its legs and finally,
by accident it seemed to Daniel, the kid turned its head
all the way around to follow a moth in the swimmy
light, and flipped over, and he and Iris looked at each
other.

He wanted to laugh, but he was held back by how
his wife was gazing at him. Iris's eyes were wide open
as if to say *What's next?*, as if anything were possible, as

if they were all going to perform fabulously from now on. He could almost believe this. It was something to see her that way. They put the baby on its stomach again and it rolled over, toward Daniel.

"She likes you better than me," Iris said. "I knew it."

Then the dusk came down fast and he had lost sight of the kid on its back in the sand, kicking its feet in silent passage.

The bus hit a pothole and shook on its back axle. He nearly bit his tongue, and made a grab for the seat in front of him. He was thinking of the warmth in his hand when he put it to his wife's neck, and then he remembered his blood was missing something vital, which made it no good to servicemen or anybody else. The Memphis Air flyboy turned around and glared at him.

"Easy, fella," he said, glaring back. He felt like a loser, though, with those defective pints inside him.

At the depot stop Daniel climbed down, and the bus pulled away emitting jet puffs of exhaust. The depot road was littered with bits of glass, sand fallen from the builders' trucks, coils of wire, bent nails. Lengths of rebar lay rusting by the roadside. All that junk lying around suited Daniel fine. He took off his shoes and slung them, laces knotted, over his shoulder. Under the waxy streetlight his feet looked bread white and soft. It wasn't tetanus that worried him (there were shots for that); it was his nerve possibly failing. He set out, putting his feet down without looking, thinking if a nail stuck him, then so be it; he'd get the iron he needed. And if one didn't, he'd try being more of a man from now on.

He hoisted his briefcase higher, as if he were wading. He had refrigerant data and his drawings for an antislugging device with him. If the thing worked, it would keep liquid refrigerant from gumming up the compressor—using centrifugal force, same as a blood separator, which pleased him now as he thought of it. He pushed on, marching himself toward his wife and the half-dug-out cellar, and the child that flopped against his chest when he picked her up.

He passed the tupelos with their half-eaten leaves, the station man's house. Then he was on the tar flats, a stretch of undeveloped land that the builders used for a shortcut. The path crackled under his feet. On a burnt-smelling road like this he had crossed the Tularosa Desert basin in New Mexico a few years back on his way to join the army, driving Lumpy Doyle's car with its big, springy seats and the gray paint peeling off the dash. The army kept him stateside at White Sands Proving Ground, where he wouldn't get hurt.

On a weekend leave in Alamogordo he'd had a blind whore, his first whore ever; he could still see her lashless eyes. She had the longest back he had seen on a woman and no hair anywhere on her body. She was oiled, and shiny that way, and the ceiling fan was going over both their heads. The fan needed new bearings, and the sound of the flat blades revolving, the displaced air coming at the back of his neck, unnerved him. He remembered now, the feeling in him that told him if he stood, if he was even to raise his head from the girl who was pulling him down to her, wanting him to hurry, if he rose up he would be decapitated. She would get all his money! He touched his pockets and she pulled harder at his belt, the black wig listing on her scalp as his pants came off. Then the voice outside the door, telling him he was taking too long and it would be extra, and the girl pushed her hands underneath his shirt, laughing. Her eyes slipped back and forth like cave fish. "Private," she called him. She made him turn over on the mattress and slowly she pushed something, later he hoped it was only her finger, up his butt, and it was then that he'd felt himself get hard. He had wanted to, he had nearly plunged his fist into her. Instead he had grabbed his uniform, turning away so her eyes couldn't float over his face. She told him she could see shadows. He skinned out of there. He itched afterward in the places she'd touched.

He washed his hands at a truck stop before going back to base. He came in at 00:20; technically, he was AWOL for those last twenty minutes out on the black desert road. The sergeant made him scrub the mess floor with a toothbrush half the night, him and a leggy half-wit boy from Arkansas, which was okay because Lumpy Doyle had worked it out about the car, and he knew Doyle would be good for another ride out of there, when the time came. Doyle was.

He wished he knew where Doyle was now. The last call came July a year ago from a bar in Vegas. Woke Iris, three months along then; it wasn't good. Doyle said he'd bet and lost, racing that ruination of a vehicle of his. Doyle had been losing bets since craps in high school. He sounded very fine.

The whore was still there in Daniel's mind, the coolness of her hands, making the skin on his butt prickle. He walked faster, staying on the tar path that was practically a bed of nails, and he was ready, hoping, even, for a 4D galvanized to stick him, but somehow he crossed the flats unharmed. Ten minutes later he stood on his own driveway, the shoes still on his shoulder. He picked up his feet to look. Nothing, and moonlight flashing all around him.

All right, he thought. He stood at the kitchen door watching his wife through the screen. She was sitting with her back to him at the green laminate table. Smoke eddied slowly in a humid cloud above her head, so he knew she'd been in there a long time. Beyond his wife was the short, dark neck of the hallway. He listened for the baby crying in its room at the back of the house, but he heard nothing.

A fear grew in him, specific. He threw open the door.

Iris turned her head at the sound. He saw her hard green eyelids, her ivory teeth. "Supper was hours ago," she said. She gestured toward the stove where a paste of eggs and cheese lay on a dish. He cried at her, "Hello! How are my girls?" and half ran past her down the hall.

The baby wasn't moving in the crib. For only a moment he thought of it possibly being dead, and he went on remote, thinking that he wanted his goddamn supper first, if he had to know, if things had to be that way, but then he picked up the kid. He lifted it gingerly under its arms, and it sucked air and breathed on him. He groaned with relief and took it back out to show Iris, who was still in the same posture, her legs crossed tightly at the knee, her ankles twisted about each other like ends of wire.

"Look," he said. The baby's eyes wobbled. "Why is it doing that?"

"Probably she has a headache," Iris said accusingly. "She's just like me."

He looked at Iris. "I'm sorry I'm late," he said.

She shifted her eyes to acknowledge him for the first real time. "I know." She stubbed the cigarette out in the saucer. Her long hair covered her face. "I'm here alone all day," she said. She reached up and tucked a spiral of hair behind her ear.

"You could call me," he said. But he knew better. Iris didn't like telephones. She said all you got was somebody telling you something you didn't want to know.

"I sent for the plans for my goldfish pond."

The baby's head lolled against his shoulder. He remembered about his no-good blood. He wanted to tell her, to come clean, but he didn't know how.

"I can't do anything right anymore," he said.

She looked at him and it was the same slippery way as the blind girl had eyed him, that time in the desert motel.

"The baby can turn over," Iris said.

Working one armed, Daniel took the plate of eggs from the stove and got a knife and fork. Iris went into the bedroom and when she came out he saw she had washed the green junk off her eyelids and she wore one of his striped shirts tied around her shoulders like a cape. Together they went out to the back steps. They laid the kid in the driveway, and the baby performed for them, flipping over and over onto its back under the sodium light.

Boy Wonder

Daniel's ma was going cold on him—not dead, but cold. Some people mightn't like you on sight, and that was one thing. Still he hadn't known a person could go cold like that, after knowing you your whole life.

At six one morning Daniel woke to his ma rousting him, tugging his arm, her face puffy with misery. He stood up half asleep and was made to strip to his shorts. These she left him. As they passed the bathroom, he saw his father coming round on the can, the long sheet soaking in the tub; but his ma cut off that sight fast enough. Her fingers dug into the back of his neck. She steered him down the stairs and out onto the porch and sat him in the pigeon chair. It was late March 1937. The kitchen windows had dew on the inside, frost on the outside. She squeezed his neck. "Don't make your noises. I won't listen." But she left the door open—she could keep an eye on him if she wanted.

His father's trouble, that would be the drink, his ma said. But you? A sopped bed is only slothful habit. The habit had come on him again. He didn't know why he couldn't beat it for good. Maybe he was just a rotter with leaking guts. He tried going thirsty. He practiced putting himself into a dead state, which was not the same as being dead. It meant keeping so still that his muscles froze up; he was hoping for a dead man's sleep. Didn't matter. Some mornings he woke with the sheet plastered under him and quickly turning cold. He was marked from birth, anyway, having only one testicle. His father tormented him.

In the kitchen his ma was peeling potatoes; the lard sizzled in the pan. He thought of how she used to drape her arm across his shoulders, or pet his hair, while he scraped the potatoes for her. If he let the knife slip and cut him, she carried his finger to her mouth and drew out the rusty blood. He knew he was no looker: his eyes sat too close together, and he was small yet for eleven, with bristling black hair that wouldn't lay down. But she used to love him anyway, or he'd thought so, a mistake he seldom made with his father.

Most nights his father stumbled in after setting the shed trap and fell asleep on the couch, his cap over his eyes. He said the trap was for rats. Bums, he meant. There was whiskey in the shed. A long time ago he had soldiered in the Great War; now he was a post-man. He had a route in Skerry proper, on the Massa-chusetts coast. Their house in West Skerry stood on a scratch of land at the bottom of a hill. The field above belonged to Lester Goddard. Same as had loaned them the trap. A lot of Skerry land was Goddard's. "But not this piece you're standing on—that's mine," Daniel's father liked to say. When he was tanked he could be a mean son of a bitch, and Daniel kept away from him.

On the porch Daniel plucked at his shorts and drew his feet up. The pigeon chair was called so for its white crust of paint, which flaked onto his back; he didn't care. Fog was drifting over the grass in front of the woodshed. His ma was beating eggs, counting the strokes aloud. He sat gaping at the swells of fog that were passing by, a blue-gray sea of air that had come in overnight. It looked thick enough to hold him. He worried about what might happen when the bully boys passed by on their way to school. His neck ached where she had seized him. What he understood was his ma had got tired of more than ruined beds. He didn't know yet how bad off she was over his father's troubles, most owing to whiskey, one the same as his. She was counting things as she used to, only more so—number of potatoes in the cellar, crows in the yard, strappings his father gave him in a week, even staring at the fingers of her hand as though she might be missing one. It spooked him. She kept the sums in her head as if they were revelations. Oh—she was singing "Fly in the Sugar Bowl" now.

He fixed his arms around himself, and let his head drop. He was so hungry he thought the juice in his gut would eat him through. Would she let him in? The boys were coming. He could hear their used soldier boots on the road. He tried to stay where he was, stony as a Massachuset, and then he got down behind the chair. He crouched among the leaves and the empty milk and liquor bottles, getting his shorts dirtier, but it was too late—they would be on him. He made for the door. "Ma," he called.

Through the screen he could see her cooking. For a moment she did not turn and he wasn't sure she would agree to hear him. "Ma! Let me in."

She turned round and he saw not her face but such gleaming surfaces: the grease slick in the fry pan, the pearly ceiling bulb. His ma wiped the spatula on the pan's rim, wiped her hands on her dress as if she thought she was wearing an apron. Her face loomed behind the screen door and she knelt down.

"Say you won't go on doing it to spite me."

He understood her and he nodded.

"It's near every night with him," she said. "It's too

hard. I'm no martyr." She looked him over and suddenly she put her lips to the screen. "Give me a little kiss."

She made him kiss her with the wire mesh between them. Her breath was tart and damp, and when she wanted another, he backed off. Then with her mouth pressed against the mesh like a drowner's, hardly breathing, teary: "Don't you love me?"

"Yes," he said.

"All right then." She lifted her dress to dry her eyes, not caring what he saw, and then she opened the door for him. He ducked inside red-faced and ran upstairs. It was enough that his ma loved him. He was trying. What did she want? Nothing; kisses, a dry bed. What did he? Not to be a lousy bastard that couldn't do it. So they wanted the same. When he came down again wearing shoes and dry trousers she handed him a bowl of oatmeal, regular.

It was the black-ice blindness in his mother's eyes that damned him. His mother could see well enough; and yet for whole days she acted blind to him. He even looked for the milk sign of cataracts such as Mr. Goddard had, but it wasn't there. The things that were happening between them, in particular the screen kisses, had always happened. But she punished him more now, for his sodden beds, for her misery. He did what he could to make her see him, but after a time he quit. He turned his face away. Then it was all the same to him as if she really was blind.

At first he was heady with freedom. On a mild April morning he called to her from the porch steps, "Ma! Watch me," knowing she wouldn't, spread his arms, and tried to fly. He arched his back and leapt from the top step. When he bruised a rib landing in the dust below, he was startled because he had thought he could do it, fly; he couldn't see what prevented him. He decided weakness was to blame. The rib would stop paining him soon. He did eleven push-ups there in the dust below the porch.

Next day he went on practicing: he was going to be a Boy Wonder. He got up seconds or maybe minutes after a takeoff, holding on to whichever part of him had nosed the ground, grinning like crazy. He wasn't stupid. Only a fool let on hurt, and he was used to bearing up under torment. So it was with his mother's blindness. When he plunged off the porch now, it was because he believed he had a real chance to fly. He quit crying *Watch!* on each attempt. He wore a set of football pads for a cowling, boxing gloves on his hands. In the afternoon he tried dive rolls, letting forward momentum carry him until he crash-landed on his one side or the other. He was frantic with envy, seeing the crows rise swiftly from the yard, while the porch boards creaked under his weight. Still there were fine moments in which he felt practically airborne as he jumped, belly empty, shoulders pumping the short wings of his arms.

When it got dark, he smelled fish frying: smelts, he could hear his ma counting how many fit in the pan. His father wasn't home yet. She called him in to wash. He was passingly good—he brought his father's spare uniform in from the line. His ma didn't so much as glance his way. Why wouldn't she look at him? Already her own arms were buried in the sink, scrubbing pans. Fried smelts lay on wax paper on the counter, waiting for his father's teeth. He was seized with an urging to throw himself on her, and then? He didn't know. He would as soon spit in her eye as kiss her. She *wasn't* blind. When he didn't understand things he took them apart, doorknobs or bird wings, and examined their nature; it was a relief to him to know how they were made, that it took so many washers or bones and no extra. Then the rebuilding, the fitting of parts, contented him. But you couldn't take apart a person. What was happiness? You couldn't see it. Bodiless as gas, it was made of nothing, so it must be nothing. He heard his father's boots on the porch, and got out of harm's way.

When his ma called him to supper he wouldn't

answer. "Last chance!" his father howled up the stairs, and it was. They let him be. Smelts, they were having smelts for supper. He wasn't to drink water after supper at night; he had no stomach for fish. He set his clock. He was trying to stave off what would happen later, when he lost consciousness and sleep took hold. There was no savior for him, no sweet Jesus standing by.

It happened anyway. He woke to a soaked bed, his chapped legs stinging. When she came for him she was angry. He tried to say he was sorry, but all she said was "What do you want to do it for?" Her hands were red from rinsing. She held his neck and steered him past the bathroom where his father might be sitting. "No concern of yours," she told him. She counted under her breath and he didn't know why until she said fiercely, "I ought to smack the daylights out of you both." She had added up the month's worth of sheets.

On the porch she took a swipe at him, but she hadn't his father's aim; she was no good at beatings, never had been. The door banged behind her. Daniel, his sorriness turning, fixed his gaze on the holes in the screen where the flies got through, until it seemed the tiny broken wires were part of seeing, and the world was scratched. And Daniel's mother, looking past, saw that the porch wanted sweeping; how many boards, how many strokes with the broom? The boy would do it if she asked, but she wasn't going to grant him that yet.

Instead she was thinking of things they needed, such as lightbulbs and sugar, and her husband pissing it all away. *Luxuries,* he would argue. There was no reasoning with him. It was his stubbornness and his memory for cold that made him drink. This was what he had told her, and how she imagined him, half a life ago at twenty, nearly frozen to death on a muddy ridge on the heights of the Meuse, north of Verdun. The machine guns were yammering ahead. The firing pits filled with icy rain. *Half drowned, cold all the time, we'd turn and turn in our holes like dogs.* There was no comfort. At night the flare of a match could get a man shot. A lot of boys missed their mamas then, a lot of them huddled in their pits, sniffling in their sleeves. He said, plenty often, *It wasn't for chumps, that war.*

Now his cheeks were cracked, his lip sagged, and he drooled in his sleep; nobody else would want him. If he pulled too hard at his whiskey it was because there was little for him beyond delivering the mail. Well, that was fine, but what was there for her? She didn't think of Daniel—he was young, he had yards of time left.

She pinned up her hair—savagely, but she was simmering down. She beat two eggs same as usual. She caught the boy watching her through the screen.

When he asked for a kiss she gave him a proper peck. She'd gone cold herself, without noticing.

The next beating Daniel got: he jimmied the trap his father kept out in the shed. It was a steel-jaw trap. It wasn't a big one. His father had borrowed it off Goddard some time back to keep rats out of the woodpile. Its trigger pan had rusted. Still it was a beauty of a contraption; Daniel liked to set it off with a stick. See those teeth snap. Never much good at rat catching. "What are you good for?" his father asked him. "Egg eating? Leave the trap be." He hadn't meant to ruin it. He only greased it to make it bite faster; it bit the stick so hard he couldn't get the stick out. His father had whaled him for that. It wasn't so bad. He was stiff for a few days, a mark for the bully boys. Then scarlet fever ran through the middle grades at school. Hard enough to dodge a person; the fever caught him easy.

The rash climbed his legs. He itched and ached as he walked home. By morning the fever had taken a firm hold and he thrashed in his bed until his ma came upstairs. She tried to cool him with a washrag. It smelled of bluing like the sheets. "Kissing the filthy Murphy girl again, were you," was all she would say. She petted his head as if he were small, puny really. She was angry. If he slept, when he opened his eyes they flooded with light. His bitten tongue swelled in his mouth and he panted for air. His mother's bedspread covered him. Green vines were woven on the cloth in profusion; his blood spotted the roses. More ruination. His heart raced. There was his mother high above him. She wiped his forehead as she spoke to his father.

"I've piled on four blankets. Let him sweat awhile."

He flinched under the washrag; she saw, but she was worn out. She was having half thoughts: If he doesn't get pneumonia, she considered as she went downstairs. She thought again of the Murphy girl kissing her boy. It cheapened her heart. She managed to make supper for them two, husband and son—they were just alike, neither of them took to corn soup, but that was what they would get—and afterward she went into the darkened front room to hear the radio. If he called her, she wouldn't know. She took care not to dwell on this. She had done what she could.

Daniel fell into a light sleep.

When he awoke he was lying in the pit of the bathtub; his ma was gone, and the corn soup with her. The tub was full of water so cold he couldn't feel much in his arms and legs. The harsh, unbearable light burned above. His father's hands on his chest held him under. His father was trying to kill him, sure. His heels banged the tub floor as he squirmed. If his father let him up it was only to rub him with a whiskey-soaked rag, and it was all he could do to keep his quivering jaws clamped shut.

His lungs ached with cold. "I can't breathe," he whispered, his father leaning close to catch it. The hands on his chest eased up. He was given liquor: whiskey, burning his lips like a siphon of gasoline. If he drowned now it was all right with him. He was so tired he could not keep his eyes open. He heard his father call out, "Boy's come round," but his ma did not come and his father did not leave him. The barren room had got so large, the water high, to his neck. He thought he had gone and died after all, drowned in Goddard's pond. His heels banged. Where were his shoes, and the brown fish? It was his father that claimed him. His father hoisted him dripping and muddy from the tub and dried him off sweet as his ma would have, and carried him to bed. There the good dream ended. He was let go, and fell among the dirty sheets with a gasp, still alive. His father pulled a blanket over him. "Lie still. Do what your ma tells you."

He caught sight of the eagle on his father's shoulder, the mail sack that was hoisted now in Daniel's place. The sack flopped there empty as skin. It waited to be filled. His father eyed him. "Can't let the rat catcher die, can we?" He slapped his cap on his head.

"You can't guess what cold is. You been kept warm all your life," his father said, and left to do his job.

He would have done anything his ma said, but she asked him for nothing. For several days she kept away as if he were still out of his head with fever and wouldn't know her. Maybe he was. She left bowls of oatmeal on the bureau for him. She was having spells of lassitude that caused her to lie down on the kitchen floor, give herself over to the flat boards. She lay on her back and slowly spread her arms, her eyes full of tears. She thought, If he sogs through he'll lie in it; it's too hard.

When he got better, he was better, that was all. She got worse. Usually it was counting things that bore her up—the everlastingness of numbers—but now she felt herself sinking. The floorboards had to bear her up for real. It was likely Daniel would stumble over her when he came in from the yard at twilight. He wasn't strong yet. She let him alone if he turned on the tap. She stopped asking for kisses.

Get up, Ma, he wanted to say when he found her, can't you try to get up? She had given up, or gone cold on him. Maybe he was glad.

He was a good boy; but it meant nothing to him.

His father got the jaw trap working right, and laid

it back of the shed woodpile. It caught a rat every few days, sometimes a squirrel. They could eat the squirrels. His ma started keeping track again of numbers caught, which was taken for a good sign. As for Daniel, his weakness lingered. Some evenings, cleaning his father's boots on the porch, he'd feel the sudden weight of water closing over him. Sometimes the drowning dream woke him before his ma could. He was back in it then: the grasping cold, his ribs staving under his father's hands. Still it was better to wake this way than the other, to a soaked bed and maybe a beating, he would tell himself, shaking in the dark. Better than his father's muttered "—boy's a goddamn infant!" How was it the one that hated you was the same as had saved you? It was a confusion to Daniel.

One morning Daniel woke to a thin gray fog hanging over the yard. His legs were still rickety. But he wanted to fly. So he had his oatmeal cold at the kitchen table, and went looking for his pads and gloves in the shed.

There was a racket of squealing in the woodpile. A bit of hide in the trap, nothing more. Without considering it, he picked up a two-by-four. It was only then that he saw what was going to happen, although not why, any more than he knew why he was his father's affliction. He stood ready in a dead stillness that gave nothing away, and when a gray rat ran out he whapped it over its sorry head.

The two-by-four was no different from the ones his father used on him, and he knew how to swing it. Sure enough the rat went down, biting at the air, legs twitching. He thought he ought to whap it again, quick, merciful. But now the first blow was done, and he felt stunned himself and could do no more. The rat lay panting on its side; then a sugary glaze came over its eye and it died.

Daniel let out his breath. He could hear his mother singing in the kitchen. "Shoo Fly," it sounded like. He took the shovel and dug awhile behind the shed. Then, using his glove, he picked up the dead rat and dumped it in its hole. He was thinking, What if Ma was to come out and see? *Mother of God, you're a cold one.* But she wouldn't care, since it was only a rat. He stood a bit unsteady over his rat, trying to guess how blood froze, how you could just go cold one day, for no reason. He remembered the cold water flooding his ears, all his father's weight on him; but he wasn't a drowner.

He wished his father had been there, and seen him do it.

It was wrong to be killing, but he wasn't sorry. It was weakness made you sorry. Once, in the schoolyard, he had waited for the bully boys with a claw hammer held behind his back. He'd pictured himself a Massachuset chief, Philip the Red King, the hammer a tomahawk; but when they came after him he was too scared to use it. He remembered this with shame. With his father's shovel he pushed the dirt back into the hole. No, you could have no sweet feeling for vermin such as a rat was.

He shook himself with sharp pleasure. Then he ran back down to his mother's porch to practice flying, leaping farther from the steps each time, willing to fly in any direction he could, which so far was always down. His ma was still crowing it up inside. He heard her as she murmured over the stove, the tune too faint to pick out. He jumped at the air. He was lighter, even this long after the fever, but the air could not hold him. What was she singing for? The ground heaved up and took him. After a bit he got up and looked himself over, the choked blue veins at his wrists, his scraped arms. Nothing broken. He knew what to want: not too much. He had the rat to brag on to his daddy. That ought to count for something.

Life in the Air Ocean

Iris sat on the edge of the roof and looked down at her baby. It was a lump under a pale blanket in the carriage below. Earlier, it had been sleeping—this thought cruised slowly through her mind. The baby had been asleep with its raw-edged thumb in its mouth, plugged in and quiet. Iris tilted back her head. A white cloud rolled east beyond the telephone wires.

She thought of the guitar music that was humming through those wires even now. The Mexicans, again. The Mexicans who were Dan's friends from his army days at White Sands Proving Ground. She could hear their loosely strung voices whenever she lifted the telephone receiver here in Carville, Tennessee. This swell aural reception—was it for real? Probably not, but she couldn't help herself. It had arrived along with the baby. At least out here on the roof her ears weren't picking up as much. Something else was coming at her, though: a red noise. She chanced another glance over the roof edge and saw the inner lining of the baby's, her baby's, mouth. That was the red wail. She thought, Okay, I get it. The sight of Daniel's bags of cement in the driveway comforted her. When will Mrs. Acheson get home? Iris wondered, checking her watch. She saw the stab of the sun in its crystal, and her own eye, but no time. The wine bottle rocked in the gutter.

She slid her palms over the shingles and lay back (Slowly, slowly, she told herself in a soothing voice) until she was flush with the slant of the roof. The aluminum gutter ran under her knees; her bare feet dangled freely. Above her spread the watery blue. In rocketry—had Daniel told her?—the atmosphere of Earth was called *the air ocean*. She loved that. We are the bottom feeders, she thought. We need thick air, we can't survive up past the lowest layer, the troposphere. Today the heat was tropical. The air shimmered over the tar flats, and in the distance the bus station's corrugated roof gleamed. She had the last swallow of wine.

The wail receded. The backs of her knees hurt a bit where the gutter edge dug into them. Okay for now, Iris told herself. I am so tired, and why? Since the baby came I hardly finish anything. Smoke was rising from the open tar pit in the middle of the flats. And she had just scrubbed the window shades that morning and hung them over the clothesline. How could you tell timing? You couldn't. Things happened out of the blue. The starlings would peck at her eyes, she thought with a fearful startle, so she flung one arm across her face. There was a spongy softness to the flesh that she loathed, but it covered her. There were red and yellow sparks of light in her arm. Her feet drifted. She drew them back, and in her ears the Mexican voices hissed and moaned of *la infanta*, the guitar songs drilling toward her along the telephone wires. Later, when she picked up the receiver, there would be those holes, the evidence.

People said it was the natural aftermath of childbirth, this lethargy, these stray voices that came and went. Iris knew she was dawdling on the side of madness. Well, but today she was having fun, goddamn it. A bulldozer growled along a track on the tar flats; she thought of the dark roar of test missiles. During their courtship, Daniel had regaled her with the laws of thermodynamics as applied to the cooling of rocket skins, his military specialty. He mentioned latent heat when he said he missed her. When he was discharged he found the laws applied also to certain modern appliances; rocket or refrigerator, its heat acted the same. The laws even applied to love, or so he said, joking. What he meant (she would understand) was that in any open system heat always flows toward coldness.

She was naturally a bit lawless, herself. Raised in a mobile home on the burgeoning outskirts of Carville, her father a plumber, her only sibling a retardo, she had tried at first to follow rules. She had won a scholarship to the Memphis School of Nursing; and why not? Plumbing was plumbing. But she bogged down. When she'd met Daniel two years ago, summer of '53, she was twenty-six and working in Memphis as a lab technician. They got married and right away Daniel was laying plans for a baby. Her coworkers, months older than she was, reminded her that if the lab chimpanzees occasionally tossed offal at her, that was no different from the behavior of a human child. A baby, that won't be anything new at all to you, they had said brightly. What did they know?

Awakening that morning, Iris had felt the top of her head for scars. Her hair was going every which way. She was still sore in her lower regions from Daniel last night; he was forgetful, he forgot how easily she bruised, how the spring in the mattress poked through. In the bedroom mirror she saw the squint eyes of her nipples and, on the back of one thigh, a bruise like a dark coin. She examined it. There might be a face—Simón Bolívar would make a fine numismatic omen, she thought. Yes: a beaked nose presented itself. The baby's room was still as a tomb; no reason to suspect the presence of a child in this house, as Mrs. Acheson had complimented her, Iris thought, at bridge last Saturday. (These Achesons claimed to be distant relatives of former Secretary of State Mr. Dean Acheson; it was not true that he had ever been soft on Communism.) The telephone seemed to be ringing, but Iris, in the shower now, pretended not to hear as she tried to rub Bolívar's blurry visage from her thigh. The couch was strewn with library books about South America. There was talk of General Electric's opening an appliance division in Colombia or possibly Ecuador. Somewhere equatorial. Of course the Colombians would have to stop quarreling first, but that looked promising. Everyone was desperate down there for refrigeration. Daniel seemed excited by the possibilities. He was playing his Lola Beltrán records nightly, and giggling when he asked for *agua con hielo* at the table, but she knew he had no idea what a move like that meant. They whispered about it late at night lying head to head in their cramped bed. He would go first to make sure it was safe. Once things were tied down, he'd send for her and the baby or babies (he was joking). Then he told her the lost treasure story—in a volcanic funnel lake near Bogotá, beyond the reach of divers, lay the gold-encrusted bones of Chibcha chieftains—thinking she might enjoy this information. Daniel found everything enjoyable. Iris got out of the steaming shower and answered the phone. It was the library, wanting their books back. Of course, Iris told them, she could be reasonable. She might or might not renew.

In the kitchen Iris felt panicked by the eraserlike rub of blood in her heart. She warmed the baby's bottle in a pan on the stove. She shook a drop of milk onto her wrist. Then, seeking comfort, she drew from the bottle. Through the rubber nipple the milk tasted chalky. She felt warmer and sticky fingered, and she picked Ruth up. I am the mother, Iris told herself. She fed Ruth until Ruth spit up on her shoulder, which another book had predicted.

At the supermarket Iris wheeled the baby carriage up and down the green-tiled floors, listening acutely to what the loudspeaker said. She suspected the Mexicans here also. The loudspeaker spoke into her ear: *Red meat,* it said, coughing. *And banana flakes and formula.* At least it was speaking English. She told herself sternly, You're a grown woman, you should learn to drive. It's not too late.

There was no more room in the carriage, so Iris picked up the baby and laid it on its back in the meat case. She rearranged things, pushing cans and jars to the carriage's padded sides, while the baby yipped and kicked among the pork chops. Its toes glistened under the sharp fluorescent lights. The baby was smiling. Iris felt buoyed by a brief spouting happiness. She put Ruth back in the carriage, and packed her round with frozen meats—pork loins next to the baby's thighs, a whole chicken beside its head—and intermittently the baby coughed under the blanket. The flip-flops slapped Iris's feet as she wheeled up and down the aisles. For a while after the birth, the sight of meat had made her sick. Today she wanted meat and only meat. See? People change, Iris said to herself. Baby Ruth dozed. Beside them a fish eye of light swam in the meat case chrome.

At the checkout the cashier touched the cellophane-wrapped meat with ginger-red nails, squeamish. The baby cried at the temporary loss of its frozen twin. Iris curled the lip of the paper sack and tucked it down at Ruth's feet. "Hush, you greedy thing," she murmured. The electric doors opened and she pushed toward the heat outside.

Iris walked home slowly along the sidewalk. Starlings dropped from the telephone wires and pecked at the grass. Lunchtime. Iris opened a package of hot dogs and began to eat them. Wheeling the carriage, she forgot her bewilderment. I am the mother, she thought for the second time that day. She was trying not to worry so much about the future.

"We go ahead as planned," Daniel had said with regard to the cellar excavation. He was fixed on having a cellar. "This Rojas Pinilla that's running their country, who knows what he'll do next." She'd caught her husband more than once standing in the driveway with the cellar blueprint in his hands, gazing east toward the Doones', two houses up. She was starting to suspect him. There was the compelling semicircular loop of the Doones' driveway; and she had witnessed the teenage Doone sunbathing at twilight often enough. "I don't tan, I burn," Iris muttered.

When she got home, she parked the carriage by the back steps next to the cement bags and pulled out the hose to water the marigolds and the marsh cattails. Other people are selfish, she thought. Let him have his cellar. I will put in Japanese goldfish. I will clear the marsh stand and bank it with stones, and my fish will swim in luxurious circles. This way, if we don't get to one country, I'll view another. She had seen the setup in a magazine: raise exotics from the Orient right in your home. Defiantly she yanked the hose along the flowerbeds, smoking a cigarette, watering.

The baby opened its pink mouth and cried. Iris

dropped the hose and checked the baby. "You wait a minute," she said. "The world does not revolve around you." She left the baby by the steps, a rock at the rear carriage wheel, while she unloaded the groceries. The pork loins had softened a bit and Iris dented the package with her thumb, watching the meat go gray under the cellophane. Then she tossed it into the freezer where its germs would not threaten them.

In the yard crows moved through the grass like beaters. Iris picked up her baby again and felt the fontanel, let her thumb map the small pit at the top of the skull, while the baby gazed at her, glue-eyed. "You'll be smart, won't you," Iris told it. She took the baby into the house and sat with it on her knee at the kitchen table, tapping her cigarette ash into a saucer. Outside the long green grass shivered in the sun. She could feel blood backwash through her heart. The leaves of the mitral valve had grown too large in her, the doctor said; so the heart was susurrous. On the wall the phone rang. When she answered, it wasn't Daniel. Dimly she heard the guitars in the wires. The baby on her knee closed its eyes with small clicks. The baby was beginning to think about things, she knew.

·　　·　　·

Iris was still on the roof when Daniel's bus stopped on the corner. Drowsy, she watched a small blue figure bob up the sidewalk, swelling like a sponge before her eyes until she said, "Oh." It was her husband, Daniel, soaking up the air. Too much air, maybe that was why he got into such lathers. She waved, glad to see him even though she knew his briefcase was chock-full of part samples for the new Hotpoints, and not roses for her.

In the yard he dropped the briefcase and jumped for the hose, which, she supposed, was still pumping water. His head dove into the baby's carriage and blocked Iris's perfectly good view of the baby. Poor baby, Iris thought. How would its daddy like such a Martian-red face checking his own nose-breathing? I bet he wouldn't. That instant, as if she had willed it, he pulled back his head. What next? Daniel disappeared under the roof's edge. The hose quit pumping. "God-damn it," she heard him yell from under cover of the gutter. The starlings came alive on the telephone wires across the street, flailing and stalling with their wings. Maybe Daniel meant to leave her out here. Maybe he would just go inside to eat leftover tuna salad while he decided on a gasket manufacturer. Last night he'd stayed up late fondling the magnet-stiffened samples like a man in a love stupor, or one going blind. Tonight, for a bonus, he was bringing home a feeler gauge so he could test their own refrigerator door for leaks. Down below, Daniel stepped back out of the flowerbed and looked up. Well, she thought, now he'll have to check me instead.

Her thighs were going to sleep; her feet were floating away. The side of the house had disappeared. She could see Ruth asleep in the carriage, an overlooked pork loin in one corner. Hose water trickled harmlessly down the driveway. She thought of expiration dates, of library books with their bluish stampings, of the milk carton with its pinched lip waiting in her refrigerator. She had seen Daniel jump for the hose. She didn't want to understand him; but her use for language had not yet evaporated. Goddamn it! Daniel had shouted, and she understood everything. What the hell, she would give him one more chance. In the yard the crows beat the grass. Mrs. Acheson's car was coming down the road. As she turned into her driveway opposite, Mrs. Acheson's gold rings flashed in the side-view mirror. If Mrs. Acheson saw Iris, she gave no sign.

Suddenly Daniel was here, leaning out the bedroom window. The wine was finished; Iris stretched her arms to him.

"Honey," she cooed, exaggerating. "Come sit by me."

"Have you utterly lost your mind?" asked Daniel.

His teeth looked gray to Iris. He was turning gray on the inside.

"Slide toward me," he said.

Iris slid over far enough to grasp his arm. Quickly she pressed her thumb to his wrist, and sure enough he went gray, the red blood in him shrinking away. She could smell the steel slide rule in his pocket. There on his finger a Band-Aid grew its grotesque flawless skin.

He was eyeing her, searching her in that way she loved; and he did it so rarely. "Adele Acheson is a hypocrite," she said. "She keeps inviting me to the pool when she knows I can't swim a stroke." She watched him carefully, but there was no reaction.

"Iris," Daniel said in a level voice, while she noticed his marble-blue eyes, his dusky eyelids that might be a woman's with their exquisite shadows. "Iris, this can't continue. It's bad enough you sit up here like this—I can practically understand it—but you forgot about the baby again."

"Oh, can you?" she asked hopefully.

"Sure," he said. "Sure I can."

He was looking at her with what dawned on her was envy. Over what? she thought. Her head ached. He'd told her once. Over the failed flights of his boyhood, those takeoffs from his mother's porch railing by which he'd tried to escape gravity. For a moment Iris pictured him as he was then, a skinny eleven-year-old Boy Wonder in football pads (he must have sensed all along that escape was unlikely), trying to dive up. Now both his feet were flat on the ground, but what good did it do him?

He rubbed his forehead as if his head ached, too, and she saw the embedded lines of his yearning. He leaned farther out the window toward her. The slide rule dislodged from his shirt pocket and fell into the long grass. Daniel's hand, too late at slapping the pocket, caressed his own breast. Below them their child Ruth kicked and gnawed the cellophaned pork loin with her bubbled lips.

"She hasn't got any teeth," Iris said mockingly. "And she hurts me, anyway." Meaning when the baby nursed, which as Daniel knew was mostly unsuccessful. "I really have no idea," Iris said, "why, when they invited us all those nice evenings, we never played bridge with the Achesons."

"Iris," Daniel said gently, "we had them over here last Saturday."

"Oh, sure, and the Foster Dulleses too," Iris said. Then she did remember looking down bleary-eyed to see legs under a table (her legs?), long gashes of runs in the stockings, but where had that been? She had forgotten whose furniture stood in the living room. She could not picture who had won. Above her, the telephone wire began to hum in the same tone as the supermarket lights a half mile away. Days on end, Iris thought, days and days on end. When she was younger she had wanted to become a doctor. She had dissected a calf's eye, strung the vertebrae from her mother's oxtail soup. In nursing school she'd peeled the muscles from a cadaver's arm. Now a baby hurt her.

Daniel was turning away, ducking back inside the house, because he knew she'd want to come in soon, he said. So she let go of his arm. Gradually she turned her head to make sure he was watching her through the window—he was. Then she slid off the roof.

In the air she kicked—*Dumb,* went the words in her head, *try* to float. She had time to notice the appliance-blue sky. When she landed, her left ulna decided to poke out its head, see the world. She lay gasping for a while on her back in the grass. The damned Tennessee bluegrass, long spikes of it trying to grow through her spine. Daniel was gazing on in horror, still thinking she hadn't meant to do it, but what she hadn't meant was to forget to put away the last of the pork. By the time the ambulance came, she was instructing Daniel on the dual tasks of freezing the meat and diapering the baby, who was worked back up to a wail, tasks he needed to perform since, Iris thought sadly, I can't now. The stretcher bearers levitated her toward the still-wailing ambulance. She herself felt little impetus to rise.

.　　.　　.

"I will just be a few minutes," Iris said on Adele Acheson's front porch, a few days later.

"Take your time, hon," Adele said. "Arm paining you?"

"I can't tell, really," Iris said. Her casted arm weighed itself in a sling against her chest. "It hurts, but it's sort of a fun pain." With her back to the porch rail, she hoisted Ruth up one armed from the meat-stained carriage. She held Ruth tightly to her, and pressed her lips to the baby's dented scalp. The baby arched backward.

"You precious dear," Adele said to the baby, catching her.

Adele had had the whole experience of raising children, four boys in her case. But they were grown now, and Iris hoped she might not remember the unbearable rawness at the backs of one's eyes. The window shades in Adele's living room were pulled low against the late rays of the sun. Adele took Ruth back into that quiet house.

Iris turned to go. She had the library books in the carriage in a paper sack. They were overdue; it was going to cost her. She had *The Book of Knowledge* volume 3 *Cel–Cuc*, and John Gunther's travel opus, as well as a water-stained book on South American birds that by the look of it had already made one trip down the Magdalena. Her hands kept fluttering at a short remove from the rest of her, like small, tame birds on strings. What if I cut the strings? Iris wondered. What would happen? They'd fly up past the telephone wires. They'd reach the tropopause, maybe the stratosphere. I should hope, she thought. She left the carriage on the lawn and took the sack with her. At the end of the Achesons' driveway she turned left instead of right.

When she reached the road's end she kept heading north onto the tar flats, marching over the black earth. Once when she glanced back she caught sight of somebody's white bedsheets on a line. They snapped and tongued the wind, and she wondered, Did Adele Acheson have some milk and a bottle and a bottle warmer, in case she didn't come back right away.

She wondered whether down in Colombia General Rojas Pinilla had babies of his own. She would guess no, if she had to guess. Here he was the one determining all their futures, and he didn't ask her, Iris Mowry, what she wanted, or what she knew. Hardly anybody asked anymore, not even Daniel. All they were interested in was Freon 12: noncombustible, nonflammable, noncorrosive, nontoxic. It sounded ideal, she thought, her throat tightening. She tried to recall what it had felt like to be burning up for Daniel, a long time ago, before the baby.

She found herself at the edge of the tar pit. If I threw in the baby, Iris reasoned, by the time anyone found it, it would appear doglike, its eyes long evaporated. She had no peers here with whom to confer. But she knew she wasn't really going to do anything. Naturally it hurt to think, if you've just had a baby; everyone said so. Bubbles were rising and opening like little mouths at the surface of the tar. Breathers were under there.

Iris could no longer hear the telephones ringing inside the houses. Daniel was coming right home after work, he had promised her. "What I say *goes*," he liked to announce helplessly. And she had let him think so. Nearby, shovel handles jutted out of the tar, the faces of the shovels stuck fast. It would be necessary to extend an arm, she thought, in order to be saved from extinction. Maybe she was already on the wrong continent; maybe this was the funnel lake. In another country, would they still have meat, and money? she asked herself.

She fished the books out of the paper sack. She cocked back her good arm and pitched them into the tar pit one by one. The encyclopedia volume first, with its portion of extant knowledge. Landing on its edge beside the massive Gunther, the bird book rived the surface like a fin, and then, slowly, they sank. What if the library sent someone round to her house? They

47

would want to know what she had done with the dead books; they wouldn't care that in the future she would be guilty of numerous accidents. It was hopeless. She closed her eyes and looked into the darkness for some source of rescue. She was seeing again the stretcher bearers. They were running through the waving blue-grass, past her this time, with their hoses and oxygen tanks. Emergency, at the bottom of the air ocean.

Elemenopy

Mornings often smelled like tar, although other things might burn: eggs on the stove, toast in the toaster, a cigarette hole in a robe. Be good, Ruth Mowry's daddy said when he left for work such mornings. My girls, he'd call out, kissing Ruth and her mother on top of their heads when he came home. At dusk the crows cried Tar! Tar! as they tumbled out of the sky.

The Mowry house stood near last on a dead-end road, and after the dead end came the tar flats, a piece of Carville land which in 1959 nobody wanted, now the boom was over. A one-lane access road ran a hundred yards farther out to the tar pit itself. Barrels of tar, even a road roller with its giant foot (smooth as a baby's rump, Ruth Mowry's daddy said, his hand resting on the warm metal), had been forgotten near-by. On hot days the tar bubbled at the tops of the barrels, and a rippled heat rose off the flats. Ruth was let out barefoot; her father said any child of his ought to know enough to watch for nails. Tar'll keep her stuck down fast, he persuaded her mother—she won't get far.

To Ruth, who was four, a sturdy child on scabbed legs, each night arrived from nowhere. Suddenly it was close to bedtime; her parents put the lights out before her eyes. You are bigger now than you were, they told her. When in the dimness they stepped away from her, she checked her parts. Here was a gray arm. Here was the brutal hair in her eye, and her bitten tongue, and the dark holes in her head and privates. When you were born you had a strawberry birthmark, her mother murmured, here, at your nostril. You couldn't breathe right, so the doctor took it out. Ruth took to watching how her chest rose and fell. What if she forgot?

"You'd die," her daddy said one night over his ice cream.

He grinned. He held her mother's swollen feet on his lap under the table and rubbed them until her mother pulled away. Finally he said, "But don't worry. You can't forget. It's built-in, that control; it's set deep in your fishy brain."

She understood the idea of automatic breathing,

the helplessness of it, though she could not articulate how she knew.

One day Ruth and her mother were having lemonade on the back stoop when a neighbor, name of Mrs. Doone, stopped by. Doone had sharp red elbows, and Ruth did not like to be near her, or most other people. She leaned back against her mother.

"Don't." Her mother swatted at her tiredly, and sent her in for the whiskey bottle. "Be quick but don't run."

The kitchen was full of dull green light that filtered through the shades. Ruth made out the chrome handle of the refrigerator, the silvery pots and glasses in the dish rack. The shape of the bottle was here, too; it was on the counter, blocking the stove clock's eye. Outside on the stoop her mother and Doone murmured back and forth. With both hands Ruth pulled the bottle down.

She was quick as her parents saw she would be, quick legs, quick mind. The alphabet's toy words came easy: *abee seedy, elemenopy*. She understood the bottom layer, the simple parts of what her parents said: the blocks, if not the tricks they could do with words. Supper talk was plain. Daddy is an engineer, Daddy makes machines. What kind? Refrigerators. She did not like the slippery talk they spoke with whiskey. When her mother said things such as "I got a bug in my machine, too; I want him home at night," to Ruth it meant a kind of *No, no, gimme!* "I want" and "I don't want" were often clear to her, but not the rest, the wanted things. She hung behind the screen, listening. The stove eye saw her. All she wanted was for Doone to go away.

Her mother was muttering about the baby she said was in her belly. "I can't see my damn feet. I can't hardly walk a step without the floor tripping me up."

"Such won't last, Iris," Doone said. "Baby'll get itself born soon enough."

Ruth pushed open the screen door, holding the bottle fast by its neck.

"Let go now, honey," her mother said, taking the bottle, and to Doone, "Freshen that?"

Doone smiled and tried to pet Ruth's hair.

Ruth hopped back against her mother's legs, meaning to escape just so far. But the legs gave way, and she tumbled over the side of the concrete stoop. As she fell, a hand reached out and snagged her arm, and another caught her shorts, and they lowered her to the ground. "Oh, she's all right," her mother said. Ruth squatted in the driveway, just beyond.

At twilight the street lamps came on. Her mother's face stood out flat and white as a plate. Their voices seesawed back and forth until, finally, Doone got up to go home. She waved good-bye and ducked under the clothesline, Ruth's daddy's shirtsleeves brushing her shoulders.

Ruth's mother rubbed her own swollen belly and closed her eyes and smoked. The cigarette's orange coal at last flew out and landed at Ruth's feet. There was no more talk, only the night-cooled smells of smoke and tar, until her mother said in her tired voice, "Let's go back inside."

Next day was too hot; the road shimmered early on. Ruth's mother kept her in after lunch.

She built a city on the kitchen floor. First she had to decide—night or day? The sun was there in the ceiling, showing itself in the blaze of the lightbulb. She stacked baking pans for buildings. Certain alphabet blocks stood for people; the red rubber bands were balloons that showed what they were thinking.

This one thinks of how a baby got into its stomach—eaten. This one picks up the sister (Ruth picked up the saltshaker) and shakes it until the insides come out. That one rides to work on a bus. Here is a rabbit in the grass; here (bit of electrical tape) a crow. These are the telephone wires singing with headaches. These are the refrigerators holding the cold food. Here is me (Ruth gave the shaker a rubber band) on my tricycle. Here is me finding Daddy's money for him in his pocket. Here I am falling down.

Now it is suppertime, and the crows have flown home, and the eye in the stove sees you while you play. Your mother has gotten up from the couch and is standing by the sink, just waking up. Her eyes drift to one side, and her mouth yawns to show her egg teeth. The bottle slides from her hand and falls in the sink with a broken sound.

Ruth's mother jumped.

"I'm clumsy," she said, her eyes angled so she couldn't really see Ruth. She got the dustpan and picked slivers of glass from the white sink and pretended to hide them in Ruth's dirty hair along with her damp fingers. "Did you get cut? Look what I found!" Obediently Ruth said *Ooh* over the sprinkle of brightness found on her. The bristle brush appeared. The fire ants swept over her scalp. The windows went dark. Her mother stood Ruth on a chair and washed her hair under the faucet.

·　　·　　·

Ruth's daddy was building a cellar under his house; in fact, he bragged, it was almost done. In Carville, Tennessee, nobody put cellars under houses. He could not understand that. Everything he did made room around him. There was money in his pockets when he came home. He loomed in the kitchen doorway. He washed his hands at the sink, humming in the refrigerator's monotonous language. Ruth knelt on the stool beside him and dug his money out. He turned and opened his mouth wide for her. "Look at all this gold," he said, bending so she might examine his molars.

"Are we rich?"

He burst out laughing. "When I'm dead you can tell the undertaker to yank it all out for you," he said, patting Ruth's head. He opened the refrigerator door and basked in the coolness.

At supper he hunched over his plate; his hair waved out from his cowlick where it had grown long.

"You look like a lunatic, Dan. Get a haircut," her mother pleaded.

"I don't get you Southerners." He cut into his fried eggs with a steak knife. "Where is a man supposed to put things? There's no garage on this house either." He said this as if it were proof of some failing. He trimmed the whites and scooped up each yolk to swallow whole.

"Disgusting," her mother said. She went and put her plate on the counter, tossing back her messy hair, her red mouth around a new cigarette as she turned and leaned against the sink. "You, finish," she said to Ruth.

The cold eggs rubbed unpleasantly against Ruth's teeth.

After supper they sat out on the back steps awhile. When her mother rose to do the dishes, her daddy pulled on his black knit cap. He winked at Ruth, and she followed him and stood exactly where he told her to in the driveway, holding a flashlight. He carried two-by-fours into the cellar hole under the living room. He buttoned his collar and pulled his cap low over his ears against spiders. They nested in the floorboards above his head, a dangerous rain, he told her; black widows eat their own husbands. She shivered for him. "You see? I'm all right—go back inside now," he called from the floodlit cellar. But she wanted to hear the hammer sound—he was making the walls.

What she would remember was the three of them dancing in the living room to the loud Mexican records until her mother fell down. She would remember how exultant they were, stamping and whirling. When her mother's tangled black hair caught in her daddy's hands, he pulled her head back sharply, and kissed her neck. She was laughing when she fell, slumping heavily to the couch, her eyes rolling back. "Faker," he said. "You've got nowhere to go, Iris." But she didn't rise, so he stood over her, his face flushed, breathing unevenly. His shirt was dark with sweat. He raised her legs to the cushions and covered her with a sheet. She stiffened and rolled away from him, showing the underpants that cut under her big belly. There was spit on her cheek.

He picked Ruth up and said she was his good girl. She had never seen him as happy as he was that minute. He carried Ruth into her room and shushed her. He showed her the rabbit's head on the wall. He sucked the rabbit's ears—his fingers. "Daddy's checking you," he said, "hold still," and he hummed his soft hum. There: he poked between her tired legs. She jerked and whined when he cracked her open.

She understood nothing. These are the letterless blocks; these are the whiskey bottles her mother pulls from under the floor; this is the money she takes from her daddy's pocket. Daddy put his fire-ant finger on her, and shivered like a very cold man. She lay quite still. She watched the ceiling for the sun. It's still night, her daddy whispered. Why? Because it is. When he put on the lamp, that was when he looked scared. A little blood was coming out of her. "You fell," he said. "You fell, that's all. Did I see you? You and your mother were dancing so fast." He patted her clean with a washcloth. "Good thing I checked you," he said with his sweaty mouth. "You'll be okay."

In the morning Ruth's mother called the doctor to say Ruth had another infection. "It's the badness coming out, is all," she said into the telephone. She put Ruth in the bathtub and washed her with hot water and tar shampoo. There was a red rubber band around her own hair, wrapped tight so no one could guess what she was thinking.

The water hammered from the faucet and was shut off. "Daddy's gone," she told Ruth. "He went to work, but he left you these." She showed her paper children, the kind that came in *McCall's* magazine, and left her a towel to dry with.

The boy doll had curly hair that was coming unstuck from its backing. Ruth peeled his face to see how he was made. When she tried to fix him, pressing her thumb over his damp eyes, his face kept lifting away. She felt the sudden pump of her heart as she climbed out of the tub.

In the magazine there were not only doll's clothes to punch out, but spare arms and legs. You laid the pink flesh of a new arm over an old one. She waited for her mother to forget her. She was good at remembering. She was a breather like her daddy, who loved her. The baby living in her mother's belly was so heavy it pulled her mother down.

The habits that came to Ruth were those of quickness, and falling. She understood plain things, eggs and rectangles and rhymes. When her father sang the one about falling, *Rock-a-bye Baby,* she was never afraid. She didn't yet understand things such as jealousy, and tearing sadness.

June bugs smacked the kitchen screens as soon as evening came. Her mother whacked a head of lettuce against the sink to get the water out. The alphabet towers had toppled in the corner. The cellar door squeaked when Ruth pulled it open. "You'll fall. You're not allowed down there, so don't try anything," her mother said without turning. "I've got eyes in the back of my head, you know."

Ruth stood at the top of the cellar stairs listening to her daddy's sawing—he was home again. The lights were blazing. Lightbulbs were the color of salt; that was why moths licked them. Then the moths' wings burned. Did it hurt when that happened? No answer from the red rubber bands, or the dolls' mouths. The steps ran down to the cellar like a steep block slide, and when she looked she saw it was her turn. She felt her mother's eyes on her like a push.

"Shoo, flies," her mother said to the June bugs. What did the tricky words mean: *you'll fall, you fell.* What was falling like? Ruth tried, but she couldn't remember any other falling, only Doone's and her mother's hands picking her out of the air. The boy doll was in her hand. She pinched his flat head to keep him still, and swayed out until she lost her balance.

It was a quick, loud fall, with no thinking in it, only hard banging against the stairs that echoed in her different parts. At the end her ear struck the bottom step; her legs pointed up the stairs. Her daddy ran to her and put his thumbs to her eyelids, trying to see in. My God, his mouth said; she could not hear him very well. He felt her bones and picked her up. His nose ran. She tried to say, *Wipe it, Daddy;* no air would leave her. She could hear her mother calling her, saying, Ruth, Ruth! Want my baby, under the salt light, and she was so thirsty, but she felt no push to answer.

Off Grenada

When the plane carrying the Mowrys touched down at Pearls Airport, Grenada, Ruth Mowry's daddy said, triumphant as if he'd flown the BWIA 707 in himself, "The big silver bird has landed." (This was in April 1962; years yet to the U.S. invasion.) The hatch opened and they beheld the sun. Where are we? thought Ruth, used to Colombian rain. There was solid ground, the pitted concrete, to marvel over at the bottom of the stairs. Inside the terminal building were more marvels: coconut palms growing right through the roof, the screech of parrots. "Hear that? Maybe they're only hiding," Iris Mowry said to her daughters, hoping to see exotica. It turned out to be a recording. Surly from behaving, Ruth gave up a grin.

Daniel took a picture of them standing under the palms: his girls, Iris, Ruth, and Monica. Monica's eyes were humid from the comb's nicking. Everybody said Cheese. Spots from the flash lurked in everybody's eyes but his. From the airport a cab took them across the island to Grand Anse Beach. They rode through the jungle, past the deep gorges of the Etang, toward the hotel on the lagoon. When the blue-black cabbie smiled at Ruth in the rearview mirror, she saw gold in his mouth, more than in her father's. Yellow fringe swayed above the windshield, Jesus-on-the-cross dangled at his eye. She waited for it to hit him, but it never did.

At the hotel they were led straight through an ancient ballroom and out to their beach cottage, last of twelve in a row. The cottage was only one room, but big enough for a double bed and two cots and two chairs and a mahogany dresser. Dinner was served on the hotel veranda. Monica fretted under the tables until she fell asleep against somebody's leg. "I *am* paying attention; she's three, they do that," Iris explained to the person.

There was coconut ice cream for dessert. Ruth, who was seven, was allowed to stay up awhile. "Bet you can't," her mother said, so she had to. She licked her heavy spoon; the second hand on her father's watch swept the marks. Then she blinked. Boils, her mother was saying over her in the darkness; she was being led off to bed. We have to watch out for boils.

Yes, her father murmured. The mosquitoes droned as they came through the netting.

At breakfast the next morning, Daniel spread a map of the western hemisphere and had Ruth pick out Grenada. Of course she could find Colombia, easy; it was where they lived now—her father's job was making refrigerators work right in high altitude. To Daniel, what G.E. was doing in Bogotá, bringing appliance manufacturing to a goddamn mountain in the Andes, that was more thrilling than any vacation. Sometimes he wanted to say to his family, *You're lucky I let you tag along.* They found Tennessee, where Monica and Ruth had been born, and some places Ruth had only heard about, such as Cuba and the lepers' island off the Louisiana coast. But a map didn't tell Ruth what she wanted to know.

"Who lives in our old house?"

"Why, does it matter? Not us."

"Do you know, I can't float at all," Iris said, interrupting. She had finished inflating Monica's horse-headed ring. "I just sink."

Daniel frowned. "That's another subject entirely."

He informed them that a leper's real misfortune was not the disease but the quarantine. The lepers' island was a jail. They were stuck there for life. In fact most people were stuck somewhere; but the Mowrys were not like most people. Bogotá, their altitudinous home, was a city full of kidnappers, and yet they had some fun there, didn't they? They would go back in ten days. This was only vacation.

"What should we do today?" he asked. "Iris?"

"Find the market. I need a hat or I'll burn."

"Snorkel," said Ruth.

"Pony rides," said Monica.

They passed her the horse-headed ring.

A waiter kept an eye on Ruth and Monica while their parents stopped back at the cottage for money and other valuables. The starched tablecloth flapped against their legs in the breeze. The lagoon sparkled in the sun, and they eyed the water with longing, and kicked each other under the table with increasing ferocity. Soon they forgot everything but the urge to connect this way, shoe to shinbone. It seemed to Ruth that their house on the steep, muddy *calle* was so far away it didn't exist, and longing was useless. So she thought about the lepers. She pictured them perched on tattered couches, doing nothing, enduring the slow molt of lips and thumbs with a patience that maddened her. She thought, What about glue?

In town they bought rolls of film and Bermuda shorts and straw sun hats. In these outfits they felt like any other tourist family. Ruth balked at keeping her hat on, though, and Monica copied Ruth. Their father said, "Sun will roast you alive, girls," and their mother added, "Dark skins protect these people. Yours don't."

"I'm boiling," Ruth said, to see what would happen.

They gave her soda water. "You can swim later. Daddy and me have our own lives, you know."

This meant they were going to tour the colonial fort. The day was half over by then.

In the evening, after supper and a bit of dancing to the hotel's steel band, Ruth's father took her for a test snorkel on the beach—the moon was bright enough. Her mother stayed behind, having laughed too loud and stumbled on the way back to the cottage. Inside, she spread her arms as if she were going to hug somebody and said, "I'm having a great time, Dan," and then she leaned over in her slip and fell across the double bed. Monica was already asleep on the cot by the wall. When Ruth looked back, she saw her mother's and her sister's bodies lying on the white beds, a dark channel of floor between them.

Her father showed her how to bite the mouthpiece, and she huffed through the snorkel as they walked. They went some distance from the hotel; the steel drums grew faint. He pushed his mask up and smoked a cigarette.

"Got the hang of it? Next time it'll be for real."

"I got it, I swear, Daddy."

"Don't swear; God will punish you," he said, which was a joke. The Mowrys did not truck with God.

They were passing scores of jellyfish on the sand, stranded and dying or already dead. Her father nudged them with his toes. Why were they dead? He said he was too tired to make up a story. "Nobody knows why it happens; it just does." The see-through jellies had no bones or lungs; things like that could live on the moon.

Ruth let her snorkel dangle and crouched for closer inspection. She could see long, tangled stingers underneath one of the animals. She picked it up. This jellyfish was cold and heavy, and its stingers didn't work.

"Leave it."

"It's dead."

"Might be a Portuguese man-of-war, might have some juice left. Even dead they can hurt you. I'm not kidding."

She didn't obey, but hung on gamely, until her hand went numb. Her father took her by the shoulders and turned her around. They didn't practice snorkeling on the return march. Ruth hoped her mother would be dead to the world, as she called it, when they got back. She was, so there were no more leery whispered *darling*s or *mousy*s; her father steered her to the cots and let go.

Whole days ran together. At first no one minded the sameness of mornings spent swimming in the lagoon, afternoons given over to naps and the pulling of splinters picked up from the stairs or the veranda's scraped floor. Ruth turned cork brown, Monica darker, but Daniel and Iris simply burned. The wild birds were taunting Iris. They were flashes of green and red wings in the trees; their squabbles were constant. The binoculars shook in her hand. "The damned birds won't stay put," she complained. She read under the striped umbrella, and didn't want to be asked too many questions.

It was fun to be where nobody knew them, again. "We can behave however we want," Daniel said, although he acted pretty much the same. No kowtowing to the bosses' wives was Iris's point. She said she was sick of trying to make important people like her. She was learning to play darts from the hotel's barman, a Carriacouan.

"He's descended from French murderers!" She

felt she had to see the place, Le Morne des Sauteurs—
Leapers' Hill—where a sort of massacre had occurred
three centuries earlier.

"Better let him win, then," Daniel said.

Monica dug holes in the sand above the tide line
and was mesmerized as they filled with seepage. Ruth
ignored the few other children. (Somebody said, *Go
to school*, so you went. The bus picked you up and
dropped you off many times, before you even learned
to count. Some kids liked you, some didn't; so what.
You got dropped off and picked up some more, you
stayed away from cars and the kidnappers' arms that
reached out of them.)

Her father kept putting off the next snorkeling les-
son, saying he was bushed; so Ruth swam by herself,
holding her breath to peer through the mask. On land
she harried Monica, kicking in her ditches and crab
pools. *Be good or disappear,* said her parents' faces then,
their wheedling hands. They paid her for fetching sunglasses and books from the room, and she threw
the money in the lagoon. Later she dove for it, looking
for the veinte-centavo coins, the flash of the silver
bolivars—it was Colombian and Venezuelan money,
no good here, but she had nothing else to do. On the
fifth day her father rose from his lounge chair under
the umbrella and stretched, showing his ribs. "Come,"

he said, grabbing the snorkels. "Let's make proper use of these things."

The lagoon was shallow, and when they stopped swimming a hundred yards from shore, they could still touch bottom. Ruth took the black rubber in her teeth as he'd showed her. Ready to sink, she hesitated, and her father saw that she was scared to do it, use the tube. He put a hand on her shoulder and felt her shiver.

"Daddy's here."

Why was he talking to her as if she was a baby? She bit hard and went under. The little valve in the snorkel tube was as good as in her throat; she came up dizzy, spitting.

Once she succeeded, he said, "Now you've got it."

"I need a longer snorkel."

"You need to practice, that's all. The water can't hurt you. Has it ever hurt you?"

She glared at him. She was hoarse from coughing seawater. She wanted to say that it had.

While she caught her breath, he swam sidestroke around her, cruising past long and white bellied, his feet never breaking the surface.

"Did you know the Caribbean has barracuda?"

"Now I do."

He turned and disappeared.

Ruth knew he must be close. She made out the dark edge of the reef ahead, in deeper water; she twisted around to see the beach, and the green-and-white markers of the hotel umbrellas. They were small as the paper parasols the barman put in drinks. Where was her father? Nobody was coming. Nobody was here either. Far away on the beach dogs barked, and it wasn't until they were done that you heard them. Had he swum back? There was no wake slick. The water riffled and she lost sight of the bottom.

At once he burst from the water with his eyes streaming. He scared her, and she had to struggle not to show it. Was he crying? He wasn't; it didn't matter. What mattered was his map of the world. Anything could fool you: the gorgeous green patina of that flat sea, which hid all its beasts, the stretchy distances between where you were and land, or the horizon. What mattered was her awful, witless need of him.

"Give me a hug," he said. She threw her arms around his waist and hung on him until he gasped and pried himself loose. "Out of breath!" He hadn't used the snorkel.

Water trickled steadily out of the bathroom tap; it wouldn't turn off. "Unbearable," Iris said that afternoon, at nap time.

She looked around at the kids. Ruth was on the toilet; Monica skulked in the doorway drinking grape juice. Sand weighted their suits and crumbled out of their hair. Iris wiped their faces with a washcloth. "You're all crusty. You could go blind." She caught sight of herself, hair whipped (the damned fans blasting on the veranda at lunch), eyeliner skewed, in the bathroom mirror. "The wrath of God," she muttered. She let her sunglasses drop over her eyes and hustled Ruth and Monica along. The Carriacouan was down by a game.

"I don't need a nap," Ruth said.

"Gee, that's too bad."

Ruth started to pull up her bathing suit, but Iris reached for it, and Monica's. "Enough—you can't sleep in them too," she said. She rinsed the suits and hung them over the towel rack.

The cots were pushed together. Monica climbed on first to be near the wall, and Ruth took the outside. Their mother covered them with a sheet—the netting was worthless. "Naked little parrots. Don't talk, sleep." She kissed their necks and was gone.

Under the sheet Ruth rubbed away the kiss. She looked at her money, the bolivars rescued from the lagoon, the dull veinte-centavos. The bolivars were best, with the sharp-nosed Libertador on one side, an eagle on the other. The Libertador stared left, west, which at home meant he saw the Magdalena and the endless cordilleras. And from here? She pressed the coin between her palms and waited to feel his eye blink.

When she woke later, drowsy, the walls were striped with sunlight, and her father was holding his camera over her. The sheet was pulled down and bunched at her ankles. "Are you asleep?" he said, and he worked the camera, operating levers and dials until the flash went off. The camera's leaf-shutter jaws snapped at her. Even then, she knew she was being consumed. "Are you?" he asked again. She wouldn't give in, but played dead as he bent closer. "Ah—you're awake, I can tell by your breathing: it's irregular."

She opened her eyes enough to see him standing at the foot of the cot. He smiled, and pressed the button until the camera snapped again. She rolled away and pulled the sheet up, which proved she was awake; but she had to do it. He dug into the compact refrigerator for ice, whiskey in a glass. "I get so happy," he said, "because, you know, I'm the one who made you."

"Quit it," she said, hiding her face in her arm. Monica stirred beside her.

"One more."

"I want my bathing suit."

"Oh, all right," he said. "I can't help it if the camera likes you."

(I can feel your camera eating me, she said once to someone, years later. She said it to a man in a Memphis bar; she was drunk and feeling no pain. A pickup line, out of the blue.)

Monica didn't know any better than to sit up, blinking. Their father peered back. "Here's another subject," he said. But he put away the camera, and pulled the bathing suits off the bathroom rack and tossed them over. "I'll go tell your mother you two are ready for loading."

Ruth climbed into her suit and sat on the edge of the cot. The wet suit felt pasted on. Dampness spread on the sheet under her, its edge just visible, like a jellyfish's.

He took her back to the edge of the reef a couple of days later, at noon, to see the silversides massing. Thousands of dwarf herring and anchovies were winding together in slow motion, glimmering and moony, fat on plankton. She hung in the water, hardly moving, and watched the beautiful show. Then it was over. The light somehow failed, and the fish sped away.

Ruth followed her father into shallower water where they could stand. "Tarpon, maybe," he said, lifting his mask. (Big fish rolling in to feed could gray the water and, Daniel was thinking, for the little guys that's all she wrote.) But the sky too was darker, so: not tarpon coming, but a storm. Without sun the lagoon turned black. Ruth hugged herself and watched people scurry on the faraway beach. Lightning flickered over the ocean. "Wow," her father said, when he saw it. "We better head in."

Voices of people on the beach floated across the lagoon. They made Ruth think of the scratched records her father had at home: they twittered and skipped so you lost the words and understood nothing. A dog was barking. Sunlight broke through the clouds for a minute, and then rain was falling. Her father tipped his head back and opened his mouth.

Stilts of electricity were walking over the water. The lightning was closer, and what would happen when it reached them? She had the word *electrocution*; she knew lightning killed you dead. Maybe first it shared its powers for a second. She thought, X-ray vision? Or would *I* be see-through? How bad was it going to hurt? Of course she wondered that. "Daddy, come on." She shook his arm.

"Okay, okay," he said. "Race you in."

They swam for shore with the snorkels slung across their backs—no time for that. Unwilling to stray from her father's wake, Ruth swallowed water until she fell behind. Once, he looked back and waited for her. Once he'd said, People drown because they give up. She redoubled her kick: I'm a rocket. Now the beach was closer. She could see people folding up beach chairs. Her father was doing the crawl alongside her, his eye showing through the mask every other stroke. He spat and blew air from his mouth; and Ruth held her breath and went under. Straight ahead she saw a band of black sea urchins gliding along the bottom. Their long, poisonous spines bristled, protecting the soft mouths underneath. She pulled her stroke so as not to graze any spines. In the swell of the surf she came up for air.

Her father had veered toward the umbrella where her mother still sat reading. He was passing right over them. She was going to shout a warning: *Daddy, watch out!* or *Sea urchins!* which gave the reason. When he turned his head to breathe, she thought, he would hear her. But she lagged, and felt her tongue go soft. Her father's eye came out of the water as he took one more stroke. He was looking at the sky. The surf crashed; the water plugged her up. She floated, dumb in the waves, and watched her father swing his feet under him.

He stood up, facing the lagoon and the open ocean beyond, and his eyes widened as if he was being amazed that minute. Then he screamed and hopped in the surf. He shook his right leg, and she saw the black urchin stuck to the sole of his foot. One of the spines went clear through, the sharp point jutting behind his toes. "Goddamn son of a bitch!" he yelled, his voice high as a kid's. Ruth stayed low in the waves.

Her mother heard the first scream, and threw down her book. (One of the children? Iris thought, trying to identify the voice. The blood sloshed in her heart.) She found Monica squatting by the sand bucket. She saw Ruth lolling (*hiding* occurred to her), and then she saw Daniel jumping in the surf. "Tell me! Tell me!" she shouted, wading into the water to give him her arm. When they made it back to shore, he let go and sat down in the sand and rocked his foot.

Iris thought, Oh but he's mostly all right, which was enough, and she was glad, since she had performed the rescue. And he had quit screaming, also reassuring to Iris; but not to Ruth, who was sure her father must be looking for her. He wasn't, though. He wrapped the sea urchin in a towel so it couldn't jab his hand, too, and yanked it off his foot. The spine broke, leaving its point behind. Blood came out of him. He flung the sea urchin away and packed the towel against the hole in his foot. His arm muscle bulged.

Ruth came out of the water to see him lying on the sand all wet and gasping. He made her think of some kid she didn't like. Good, then, what happened. But it was not good of *her*; she knew it wasn't. She hugged herself, teeth chattering.

Her mother knelt by his head and passed Monica his mask to hold. Someone had gone to get the hotel doctor, who came at a trot with his leather bag. The rain stopped, and some of the other guests returned to watch. Her father bit his lip and didn't make any more noise. The towel soaked red, dotting the sand. Ruth's mother saw her standing there. "Don't you look," she said, and raised a hand to bar Ruth's eyes.

On the last day of vacation Monica rode her pony ring through the little waves. Daniel sat watching from his lounge chair (twin to his wife's) with his foot propped up, a bamboo cane, slices of mango arranged on a plate. He had dragged the chair to the water's edge—he would be closer that way, should anything happen to Monica. Iris was with the barman. Daniel didn't concern himself; it was innocent, just darts and a little island rum, which she had come to tolerate. And Ruth, off by herself down the beach—he kept one eye on her. They were resting in their little war.

There had been arguments between him and Iris. He didn't blame Ruth for what had happened. She hadn't understood the danger. He doubted she had even seen the sea urchins.

"Oh, she saw, all right," Iris insisted.

"Let's ask her, then. Ruth——" He hunkered down and took her hands so she couldn't get away—his Ruth. He asked with mild, sad-sack eyes.

"I'm sorry," she told him, teary.

He squeezed her hands. "I know."

"That proves it," Iris said.

"That proves nothing. She's a little kid. I should have looked out for myself."

There were delicate surgeries to be performed with tweezers and hot needles as bits of the urchin spine worked their way out. He was infected. The doctor came to lance the foot daily and re-dress the wound. At night Daniel moaned.

Now, on the last afternoon, the doctor was crossing the sand. Daniel asked Ruth to hold his hand and keep him company. Don't look, he told her this time. It's just the same as yesterday, more bloody pus. But she had to watch; it's how she was. During the iodine wash he crunched the small bones in her fingers. Even the doctor looked up with raised eyebrows. The sun was so hot.

"I can't dig too deep," the doctor said. "You understand it would only cause worse injury."

Ruth's father closed his eyes. "Go on, have your swim," he said to Ruth as he released her. Sulfa was dissolving at that moment under his tongue, and so his thin smile. He was ready to leave this place—he was glad not to be a leper.

Ruth waded out into the lagoon. Was he watching her? He said he would, but he wasn't. He was eating the mango. He was dangling slices for Monica, who nipped at them like a pony. Already he had forgotten her.

She swam around in a kind of frenzy, showing off little explosions of speed until she was tired. The sun beat down, fading the island shore. Her father sat in his chair. She picked him out by the knob of his bandages, and then lost him against the salt-colored sand and the glittery sea. *You did not make me*—she was going to shout at him, when she found him again—*I made myself!* (Without wanting to, she would also ask him, *Do you still love me?* and shiver, and wait for his pat on the head. *Yes.*) She swam some more, straying out so far that her father got up and waved at her to come in. She hung in the water and listened to his taxicab whistle. They were all going home tomorrow. Her name floated across the water: Ruth, Ruth! It was hers, but she didn't want it.

Cloudland

In her pajamas Ruth Mowry stood tall at 8,660 feet (plus her own forty-six inches) above sea level: this was Cloudland. She was standing on the wide mahogany doorsill of a house in Bogotá, a house inhabited by Mowrys for the past three years. Here on the altiplano, living on thin air, they were prisoners of altitude. It used to hurt to breathe. She was seven now, pent up. She still got nosebleeds when she charged the yard walls, racing full tilt across the grass and veering off at the last moment, but that was all. She hardly remembered her earlier existence.

She knew what a caul was: a scrap of water sac, a ward against drowning, nothing more. Her mother had not preserved the one she was born with. She slept burrowed under the green blanket. When her eyes opened, when she put her head out into the cool air, she felt her scalp tighten. The caul, grown back? She got dressed for school in the plaid kilt with the crossed straps, in the shirt with the elf embroidered on one shoulder, in her glasses and heavy red shoes. A comb was dragged through her hair to pull out the tangles. Belén, the maid, walked her to the bus stop and put her on the bus. The bus let her out inside the school's compound, where she reentered the perpetual shared day of second grade until they said, Go home. She was rarely left unguarded.

She had a tongue, and fists. She was like any other kid who exposed the knob-and-socket joints of dolls, or used a lens to set leaf fires in the schoolyard. She was the same as that kid, and for the same reasons: boredom and temper. Reasons as familiar and unfamiliar to you as your own. Her father drew a blue eye on his thumb with a pen. See? He was checking her with his fingers. *Sale sangre,* a little blood might come out of there, he whispered, don't worry. Her mother, lost in a trance, scrubbed her clean in the tub, and Monica the same. When her father stopped checking her, for a while and unconsciously she quit her usual head banging. Monica went on eating dirt; who knew why. Not teachers. Not their mother. There was a lot nobody knew.

This morning they were in *el mar de nubes,* the sea of clouds. Ruth watched a low cloud drift through the garden. Her father's chicle tree vanished, and when it reappeared its bark was wet and black. Farther out nothing could be seen; the walled yard, the iron gate, even the front hedge, were gone. You—you were sure you existed. Other people seemed the same when they came back to you from fog, but how could that be? Her bare feet left prints on the brick walk. She was here, anyway.

Her father came outside with his robe open, rubbing his chest. "Notice anything different?" he said.

"It's too foggy."

"Not even going to try? You're no child of mine."

But she was used to him.

He hauled out the ladder and set it against the yard wall, near the front gate. They climbed until they could look over. There was the familiar cement street, its cratered surface just visible. Unfamiliar, the barbed wire inches from her face. Six taut strands, anchored every few feet to metal posts set in mortar, ran along the top of the wall. Tangles of wire festooned the top of the gate. Her father plucked the wire; the barbs quivered. "Hear that? They buzz," he said. "Let's run a test. Give me your hand."

He mixed a little pain, a little awe, into his lessons. She was used to that, too. She wasn't scared when he leaned against her, his long body covering hers, when he said *Don't fight me* to her ear. Oh she was on the cement moon now. It was a place that existed in memory, like Tennessee, the place they'd come from. She forgot the real place: it had a raw concrete floor, a damp smell, but she kept forgetting where it was. On this moon there was no atmosphere, so no breathing. It was very nice not to breathe, not to feel the thin gas in your lungs, no coughing. Why did we want oxygen? It wasn't so bad here.

Her father held her hand to the barbed wire. "Ready?" he said, and he applied a certain pressure. In a second she was suffocating inside her skin. Her father wouldn't let her up until the test was done. She counted backward with him, three-two-one to takeoff, when a barb penetrated the meat of her thumb. She flinched. She wasn't a crier.

"Isn't it pretty," he said.

The barb, or the animal blood that was leaving her? He smiled and answered before she asked it.

"You."

"You guys think you're such pals." Ruth's mother came outside, barefoot, drinking orange juice. The top buttons of her blouse gapped open. She went into the ivy bed, and turned among the crèche figures, which were covered with soot—it was May. "I'd say these dummies are better company." She knelt and tried to soothe the trampled ivy, ironing the leaves with her hands.

"What's that supposed to mean?" Ruth's father said. "We're done, Ruthie. Go wash up." He shooed her from the ladder.

Monica was squatting by the hawthorn near the front door, putting dirt into her mouth. Monica's eyes widened. "I need my *bebé*," she told Ruth with her black tongue. The Jesus doll in the crèche, that was what she wanted.

"You put it there," Ruth said. "You can't take it back."

Their mother was shouting in the ivy. "Why'd you up and leave the table like that? I'm here too, Daniel. You can't just ignore me!"

Monica drew a shaky breath. Ruth looked back and saw her mother's fist swing, and her father catch the blow before it landed. Slowly he opened her fingers, and held her hand flat against his chest.

"Iris," he said in his patient voice, "if I was ignoring you, I wouldn't have seen that one coming."

Monica had gotten away. Irked, Ruth made out her faint track in the dirt. The thinning fog could still dissolve you; Monica's trick was she didn't need fog. Their parents loomed up, hair bristly with dew.

"I need some fun, Dan," her mother was saying. "I need to go someplace, see somebody. Otherwise I'm stuck."

"Okay, that's doable." He scanned the yard for

Ruth, who had stepped backward into the dark house. "Who wants to go for a ride to the waterfall?" he called.

Inside, Ruth edged toward the stairs, where Monica's face was a target moving between the spindles. "It might rain, Ruthie," Monica said in her odd, low voice. "My *bebé* might get ruined."

"Too bad, then," Ruth said, closing in. Automatically she pulled back her fist to sock Monica.

"If I'd re-upped in '54, you can bet we'd be someplace worse," Daniel said to Iris, who was tired of rain. The fog, at least, had lifted. They were in the Rambler, going for a ride to see the Tequendama waterfall. "Some people think sixty-eight degrees Fahrenheit is the ideal temperature."

"Not for me." Iris went back to reading the newspaper.

There had been another kidnapping. The Reds—probably it was them—took a Texas Oil vice president's boy and ransomed him for fifty thousand U.S. dollars. He turned up later, alive but frostbitten; they'd kept him in a walk-in freezer. She read the article once and then, since the kids were in the rear bay absorbed in comics, she read it aloud to Daniel.

"That was smart, using a freezer," he said. "Wish it

hadn't been one of ours." The G.E. refrigerator factory, like the Texas Oil refinery, was supposed to be a showcase for the Alliance for Progress. "*Son gente muy malos* we're dealing with. It's the industrial frontier." But he was feeling lucky. He got to be alive, too, on the roof of the world.

At the edge of the altiplano the road turned into a series of switchbacks dug into the side of the mountain. There were no guardrails. One prayed to the Virgin before descending. Cement crosses marked the places where cars and buses had gone off the cliff. "Whoever built this didn't know much about banking a road," he said. He hadn't shaved. His neck was sweaty. "You girls all right back there? Monica? Pipe up if you want me to stop."

"If a bus goes off the cliff, does everybody in it die?" This from Ruth, who'd felt the car lurch.

Beside him Iris turned her face into the wind and murmured, blue smoke streaming from her lips. He was sure she was praying for them. She couldn't quite shake the habit.

"Even the babies?"

"You betcha."

"And after?"

"There isn't any after."

"Nobody knows for sure," Iris said.

When he stopped the car a while later, they were

all drowsy and a bit carsick from the pungent smells of eucalyptus and burning motor oil. They were near a cinder-block shrine. What now, did he want to light candles? asked Iris, in shock.

"No, there's a dog in the road. Don't let Monica see this." He got out to look. Ruth climbed down over the tailgate.

The dog was still alive. Its eye rolled around, trying to keep them both in sight. "It wasn't me," he said to it.

It was black with matted fur, a medium-sized beast. It had a torn belly, and he thought twice about letting Ruth see, but as usual she was right behind him. "Well," he said, "you're here now, help me drag it off the road." It was heavier than either of them thought a dog could be. There was so much blood, and flies. Black jelly leaked from under its tail. The dog tried weakly to snap at their hands.

He wiped his face with his handkerchief. "Look," he said. "I have to put this dog out of its misery."

Ruth said, tears in her eyes, "Take him to a doctor."

"There aren't any doctors. What else can I do?" he asked. "What? Tell me." At his feet the dog's legs jerked. Dog trying to run, that was an awful thing for her to see. She was suffering too. He was a fool; his guesswork was off, it wasn't going to be an easy passing. He shouldn't have let her get this close. Condors, those murderers, were floating in the sky.

"Don't fight me, okay? I'm not the bad guy," he said as gently as he could. He went back to the car.

Iris opened her car door and said some words to him that he couldn't listen to. He shook his head; that was his answer. Monica climbed out with a fork to dig in the dirt. "Stay with Mommy," he said, and reached down to pat her head. Then he got the shovel from the rear bay.

The black dog had quit trying to run. It wasn't really a dog anymore, he told Ruth, it was just a part of the road. He could see she was going to hate him—for how long? There would be no absolution. His hands were shaky. He raised the shovel.

"Close your eyes."

"No." She was crying. "Why don't you hit me!" she yelled at him.

But he never hit her; her mother did that.

When the shovel struck, he knew, her eyes would show her the dog's bitten-off tongue, its loose black lip, but not the rest if he could help it: not the black head split just behind the ears, or the back of the shovel.

"Suit yourself," he said.

·   ·   ·

The park official said he could tell them certain things. The river above was the Bogotá, a tributary of the Magdalena. At 140 meters the Tequendama was Colombia's highest waterfall. A giant had made its deep crater with his walking stick, many years ago, when the earth's crust was molten.

"Oooh," Ruth's mother said, clapping. The water was falling with such enormous force that mist boiled up like steam into their faces. The park official mopped his face with a stark white handkerchief and said they must understand that volcanic rock was soft and full of infinite tunnels; and that in the last year alone four people, thinking that water was soft also, tried to swim across the crater. They were battered by the falls until they drowned. Their bodies were never recovered. Where the endless water came from was a great mystery. "From rain," Ruth's mother shouted. Ruth didn't believe that.

Despondent, Ruth went off by herself to the far edge of the platform and hooked her arms through the rope fence. She tried to think not about the black dog but about the underwater tunnels instead. (Her mother saw that no one could reach her, and there wasn't time now, really.) She took in lungfuls of the damp air until her chest hurt; she listened to the water roar. Where did the infinite tunnels end? Her father said infinity wasn't a place, it was a property of numbers. She didn't understand that. Maybe infinity was at the bottom of the bottomless crater, where the drowned people went. The black dog, too.

"Your father is going behind the waterfall," her mother said, tugging her arm. She let herself be taken back to the others. More people had arrived, and swarms of mosquitoes. A man wearing polka-dot shorts made room for her at the rope. "Follow the parrots with your eyes," the park official said. "See? There's the path behind the water. Soon you will see your loved ones." Time went by, and more time. When her mother swatted the mosquitoes, Ruth said, "Don't. I want to feed them."

"Well, keep them off your sister, while I light my cigarette."

Monica, beside her, was hypnotized by the water. Until now she had loved only dirt. Welts were rising on her arms and legs. Ruth didn't care; her sister deserved to be bitten.

Their father was waving at them from the ledge, reaching out to dip his hands in the plummeting water. She thought he might slip and fall, even that he was supposed to. What would happen to him then? She pictured him facedown in the dead man's float, his hair fanning out in the water, same as when he taught her that float in the pool at Girardot. The dog's blood would wash off him, the dust and even his money, and then the crater would swallow him, if it was the way people said. She would hate him as long as she could. She would not do what he wanted again.

The worst was to fear for him anyway. When a log drifted by, she cried out, "What is that?" Her mother hushed her. The park official, proving his good nature, sent a boy to the lower platform with a net. No bodies rose.

Her mother licked her lips and set her face in a smile.

Her father came back soon enough. "That was dazzling! I got to see the world from inside out. You should have come with me, Iris."

"That's sweet, but I haven't lost my mind yet. You were teasing death, I saw you. Can we go now?"

"I was waving to you," he said. "You were all as still as statues."

A few days later Belén, the maid, carrying needles in her hem for protection, walked Ruth home from the bus stop. This was the usual routine; no kidnappers appeared. Ruth's mother had her head down on the dining room table. Her wet hair was leaving ashy water spots on the mahogany. Ruth touched her shoulder. She raised her head. "Is that it?" she said. "Come give me a kiss." She quizzed Ruth on subtraction before sending her out to play.

It had rained earlier and the high cement walls were steaming as they dried. The long grass flattened under Ruth's feet until she tired of running back and forth. The seesaw was broken. She planned to lie on it anyway and look at how the barbed wire carved up the sky. But as she slowed down she saw the shovel, its plate dirt-cleaned, in the corner of the garden. There was nothing to do then but wait. For what, for her father to come home? The crèche figures in the garden stared out with their hooded eyes, their skins streaked with soot and rain.

At five her mother appeared on the walk with a tarnished flask. "The ivy's growing back," she said, putting her lips to its neck. "Finally."

Weeks ago, Ruth's father had torn the ivy down from the side of the house. He piled the vines on the stone barbecue, doused them with gasoline, and lit a match. "See how ivy is shaped like hands?" he said. "Ivy will pull a house down." Ruth felt the whoosh as the gas fumes caught. The vines twisted in the fire, spitting sap. Her mother watched from the dining room window as the hands of the ivy burned. They could hear her muttering and cursing, but she didn't come outside to stop him.

In the garden Ruth wiped the soot from the crèche Mary's nose and mouth. Breathe, dummy, she wanted to say.

Her mother dug weeds with a trowel. After a while, she called Monica to the ivy bed and let Monica grub. She sat back on her heels and had her whiskey while Monica dug up everything. "I can't get that dead dog out of my mind," she said to Ruth. "Remember Blacky?" Blacky the dachshund, given back to the *finca* man within a year of his bestowing.

"You didn't like Blacky."

"I can think of him, can't I? I don't like animals with teeth."

"People are a kind of animal."

"Well, I don't like most of them either. What happened to the hummingbirds? Where's your father?" She squinted at her watch.

"I don't care," Ruth dared to say.

"Watch out, I'm in no mood." Her mother got up unsteadily. *Getting her legs under her,* she called it. "The green-breasted ones, they fly hundreds of miles to get to our hawthorn. Everything they need is here. Why they would leave is beyond me. I'm going in."

In the dusk Ruth felt the night breeze slipping over her head. She thought of her caul and wished for it, for some kind of helmet. It was Belén's night off, and her father was the one who was going to fix supper if he ever got home. She was hungry. Maybe he had to test more refrigerators. Maybe his fingers were freezing cold. She saw a hummingbird fly in over the barbed wire and drop straight to the hawthorn, same as before.

The dining room chandelier went on. Ruth spread her arms as if she had wings. The rich chandelier light hurt her eyes, and she looked away. The grass was slippery.

Her sister was bobbing toward her. "Can we go in? I want to go in." She took Ruth's hand.

"We can't yet."

"How come?"

"She's in a bad mood, we have to wait." Ruth studied her sister's dirty fingers. What color blood might come out? But you could never get the blue kind. She shook Monica off her. The hummingbird was just a blur in the dusk. The hummingbird, and lots of other things that she was half aware of: the slippery grass, the growl in her stomach, the tremble in her mother's legs, the dog's black jelly, the oxygen gas that there wasn't enough of—something was the same in them all. Something blurry or like a blur. You couldn't hold on to those things. She looked around in the half-light. She thought of the dogs gone to infinity, which wasn't a place, Blacky, and the one in the road. Suddenly she was grieving, and wild in it, not knowing any other way to be. She turned and charged the front wall.

Thin, harsh, the sooty air in her throat, her lungs. Her barrette came unsnapped as she ran. She was losing the wall. She chased what she could see: wall and air mixing, becoming the same. There was the iron gate on one side, the embedded pulley with the bit of clothesline on the other, concrete straight ahead. Behind her Monica cried, "No, don't!" The high wall loomed up, a tower, no sea of clouds. She lowered her head and ran as if she meant to smash through to the other side. She didn't care if she broke her neck.

It was a bad crack-up. For an instant she felt herself plunging into thick blue shadows. Then the towering wall seemed to turn and roll like a wave, and throw her backward. Nothing but falling for a long time. It was work to swim up from that dream. She woke with a bloody nose and hurt through in all her parts. She was sick in the grass. After, she didn't move much; no thoughts came to her. When she heard the whir of a hummingbird's wings, she went to grasp its pulpy heart. She cried when she missed. Monica was squatting right beside her, pulling on her hands. The light from the house had washed away. "Get up, Ruthie," Monica cried, too, as if she was the one whose caul was gone.

.   .   .

When her father came for her, his flashlight illuminating the incoming fog, he said, "What's the first rule of survival?" While Ruth figured out how to talk, he straightened her limbs. She felt her legs jerk.

" 'Try, try again'?" she got out.

"No," he said, smiling. "Breathe. That's all." He checked for broken bones. Only that; no eyes on his fingers.

He carried her inside and put her on the bench in the front hall. The overhead bulb was blazing, giving him a sharp blue outline the same as the door frame. He petted her hair. "Good girl," he said. "My God, where'd you get an idea like that." He fed her milk with whiskey in it. When she breathed, it hurt so much she wanted not to breathe at all. Her father rubbed her feet and kissed her forehead. "I thought I told you, there is no after," he said. "And if there is, you don't want to go there. Believe me."

Ruth's mother sat at the dining room table, blinking, stuporous. She needed coffee; he brought her some. "Come on, Iris, try." At first she resisted. He held the cup to her lips and made her drink it. "You need air, too." But she was choking.

Ruth tried to struggle up.

"Both of you, stay put," her father said. "Doctor's coming."

She held her breath. She had always believed him.

The State of Union

Iris was hanging the wash behind the house in Carville when one of her suspicions suddenly cleared like running tap water. She was stringing up Daniel's undershorts, and as she examined the sagging elastic waistband, somehow she knew. Daniel had been unfaithful. Iris kept moving along the rope line regardless, fastening pins. She saw that she had pinned Daniel's clothes upside down. The collars of his shirts dragged in the dust, and his trousers plunged waist first into the dry grass as if some fool had done a nosedive off the roof. She hung his blue jeans: now two guys ate dirt. Socks lay scattered over the grass like feet severed in a car wreck. Up in the trees the crows were raising Cain.

Iris peered at the sun, her forehead damp with sweat. She felt nauseous. This time the girls weren't here to tell her, right to her face, that she was nuts.

They were out on their own—Monica away at dirt school (Florida State Ag and Tech), Ruth working in a diner on the other side of town, last she heard. Who would help her? She left the dog, Jack, staked out on his short chain and went back into the house, meaning to lie down. Instead she had a shot of vodka from the bottle in the freezer. Then she lit the stove. She stared at the blue flame, her stomach icy, and tried to hypnotize herself out of what she was thinking.

In the yard Jack, a mutt with crispy fur and a collie nose, was scratching a hole. Iris could see him through the kitchen window. She hadn't got it in her to stop him. She didn't like staking him but he had a tendency to roam. He had been known to return with chicken feathers on his smiley lips. "Jack's going to get himself shot," Daniel said the last time. But he believed every dog had a right to a dog's life.

So a certainty came to her: Daniel was unfaithful. He was sleeping with other women—probably there was one in particular. She tried to concentrate on the stove flame. The blood splashed through her heart. How did she know? She knew. She had felt her skin turning into another woman's skin; it was turning on her even now. She looked down at herself, at the raised mole on her forearm. In certain places her skin was blotchy and red, as from below that other skin blighted this one. She knew the biological facts:

the inner epidermal cells migrate slowly toward the outer surface; the visible self constantly is being shed. But this was different. Iris could feel the other woman's skin growing in the places Daniel had touched.

The blue stove flame sputtered. The itch maddened Iris. She scratched at her arms. She thought of hurling the mattress out the big upstairs window. She pictured her fleshy arms outstretched, the heavy mattress split open in the yard. She would soak it with gasoline! Abruptly she switched off the stove. The hypnotism wasn't working. She didn't want any lunch, or any more of the freezer vodka, for which she would have to answer. Vodka was what Daniel drank; she never used to like it. She had always drunk whiskey, after her daddy. She pulled another bottle from its nest inside the vacuum cleaner, and sat down to think.

The doorbell rang. Through the window she saw Jack lunge, yelping as the chain caught him up short. The rapist is here, she thought. Iris believed that every woman's rapist appeared in good time. Today she felt unlucky, and mean on top of that. She went to see who it really was. As she passed the telephone stand, she happened to notice the Chinese calendar hanging on the wall. It was a free gift from a take-out joint in downtown Memphis, miles away; what caught her eye was 1976/July's photo of the Forbidden City. Only a few months ago, the dogged Nixon had gone back to China. He was another Northern liar, and yet, even in disgrace, he was a necessary man. She imagined fawning Chinese women leaving lipstick on the ex-president's collar. In the photo the city's walls rose ominously behind fluttering red flags. Her own sister's birthday was tomorrow. Can't be her, Iris thought. That's something, at least. She let the meter man in to read the meter.

In the afternoon she fell asleep on the couch while watching an old war movie on TV. The South Pacific was in flames. The screams of the dying sailors were reassuringly theater-of-war-like. *We're not really dying,* they said to her, *couldn't holler this loud if we were really dying.* When she awoke she half expected to see all twenty-seven bones in her hand—that anatomic number popping into her head as handily as if she had finished nursing school all those years ago—the flicker coming off the TV was that strong in the dark. She struggled to sit up. The news was on; President Ford was back from some junket. It might as well have been Nixon coming down the steps of *Air Force One,* that hounded smile on his lips. Automatically she picked up the vodka bottle, in case there was a swallow left. She expected nothing from Ford.

The phone rang in the kitchen. Monica, calling to tell her, again, exactly what dirt was made of? The floor in there was linoleum tile, the top layer scratched and peeling, and she hated to spend too long on top of that floor. She picked up the phone. It was Daniel. She remembered she had left his clothes flapping outside on the line.

"How about Chinese?" he said from far away. "I'm kinda in the mood for shredded pork, you like that. Or crispy duck. What sounds good?"

"Oh, like you're coming straight home," she said, wrapping the phone cord around her finger. Where was he? She listened for background noises, but there weren't any—he could be in China himself for all she knew. Her finger swelled. She unwound the cord and watched in fascination as the crimped flesh regained color. "I suppose I'm too dumb to notice how late you'll be."

He was cautious. "What's the matter with you?"

"Nothing," Iris said. "By the way, is she anybody I know this time? One of our close friends or neighbors?"

"Is who anybody?"

"You make me sick, Daniel." What did she expect? She had married a man whose aim it was to make the world a colder place. First red meat and ice cream, then spent nuclear fuel rods, it was all cold storage to him. He was calling himself a *safety* engineer now; it was ridiculous. He would never answer her truthfully. In her own way she relied on that. At least right now, while she was too groggy to continue this line of questioning.

He said nothing. She heard him sigh. He was only half trying to defend himself. There was one more thing she wanted to mention.

"President Nixon was on TV."

"Nixon? You mean Ford."

"Nixon! With lipstick on his collar!" she shouted, unable to remember more. Her head was taking a nasty hammering. She knew she had seen something. "Don't think Pat doesn't notice. You're all about as bona fide as a Virgin Mary." But she meant to say *Bloody*, not *Virgin*; the drink was a fake, not the icon. Despite her heretical leanings, she gasped at the way it came out.

"Let's start this over," Daniel said after a moment.

"Oh, come on home whenever you feel like it. Your frigid wife will be waiting."

"You're drunk," Daniel said patiently.

"Okay, yes." It was such a relief to find this out that she sat down on the ugly floor. She laid the receiver down on the linoleum, and let it cry.

·   ·   ·

Daniel pretended to be sleepy so Iris would come lie down with him on their bed under the alcove window. Her mood had seemed improved by the hot take-out food. He shut off all the lights except for the one over the aquarium. This was a fluorescent bulb built into the hood, and it gave off a soothing violet light that lit up the water and made the shed fish scales glitter like diatoms. The fish, two gourami and an angelica, swam through the haze behind the bubbling filter. Daniel propped himself up on one elbow and tried to kiss Iris.

At first she went along, but after a minute she felt her lips go numb and rubbery. "What's wrong with your mouth?" Daniel said in a jokey tone. He pinched her lower lip between his fingers. "Baby," Daniel said. "There's only you." He tried to push his knee between her legs. She quit kissing him. The other woman's skin was taking over. Iris felt herself being stuffed down inside it, and, like a taped-up kidnap victim, she couldn't make a sound. She felt miserable. *How could you do this to me?* she asked Daniel with her eyes, but he couldn't hear her. He put his hands under her shirt, but she, Iris, wasn't wired up to that other woman's breasts, so nothing he did worked on her. In a little while Daniel rolled away and made groaning noises. "I'm not a pervert," he said. "I don't enjoy it when you play dead."

Even her hair seemed dirtier to her, as if that other woman hadn't gotten to the beauty parlor. And yet she felt sorry for him for a minute. He hadn't bothered to finish his crispy duck.

The next morning Iris stopped at a toy store in downtown Memphis to see what she might bring her sister Faye: boomerang, dump truck? The only thing she could find that might work was a rattle, so she bought that. She had left the car windows rolled up because she would only be a few minutes, but when she emerged with the rattle in a paper bag, Jack was drooling. He dug crazily at the backseat, his claws scoring the vinyl. It had been a long time since he had been anywhere in the car. When she unlocked the door, Jack got loose and ran in circles around the parking lot. It took a box of Milk-Bones (with a picture of his collie mother on the front) to bait him back.

At the gate Iris asked the guard for directions to Building 19, and it was where it had always been. There were bars on the windows, although the residents were low-grades. Iris parked the car and sat with the rattle in her lap. She was wearing Daniel's old brogans, which she had pulled on when the meter man showed up yesterday; now she could not give them up. Without socks they were loose, though; her toes groped the insoles. She hated Daniel. "Stay," she told Jack. She tied his leash to the steering wheel.

On the ward she found Faye having snacks in the dayroom with the other residents. The ward charge, a fiftyish Czechoslovakian named Mrs. Zdráv, brought Iris a plastic chair, and they sat in the doorway. Iris spied Faye, who was circling the room rapidly on her elegant, narrow feet. "How has she been?" Iris asked.

"Oh, fine, fine. Faye like to pinch woman's bosoms," Zdráv said. "We have to watch her alla time." Zdráv had a square head like a chunk of concrete and tiny gray eyes. After a while Iris elicited the details of a recent eye-gouging incident, set off when Faye was seated too close to another resident at lunch. The eye: saved. "Now she learn sign!" Zdráv beamed. "I show you. Faye!"

As a child Iris had earned small bribes (potato chips, hamster) for coming here. Now, although she knew better, she yearned for the big reward: her only sister swiveling her head around to exclaim, "Iris!" But no such thing happened. Instead Zdráv hoisted herself up out of the plastic chair and towed Faye over by one arm. Then Zdráv made the juice sign: a thumb tipped toward an open mouth. Faye wagged her head, shrieking. Zdráv beamed and gave Faye another cup of juice. "You see?"

Iris nodded sadly.

"Would you like to take her to toilet?"

In the long, pink-tiled bathroom Iris led Faye into a stall and sat her down and pulled off her Bermuda shorts and underpants. Faye bounced up. Faye, bones with a thin pink hide pulled over them, forty-two-year-old female phenylketonuric, had gotten along all right up to the age of one, when the irregular metabolics of her brain betrayed her. Faye had always been a pincher. Also, she lacked speech, although right now Iris believed Faye knew full well (same way a dog knows things, by tone of voice) what "Sit down, damn you" meant. Iris sat her sister down by yanking on her arm; Faye bounced up. Iris pulled the orange stall door shut on the both of them. Faye rocked from one foot to the other until Iris put a hand to her sister's flat chest and shoved. Her sister landed back on the toilet, letting out a squeak like a dog toy. Iris pressed on the top of her head to hold her down. She checked her watch, startled to see that it was almost four. She imagined Daniel heading home tonight from Oak Ridge—he was a government darling since he'd thought up the cooling fins for G.E.'s IF-300, a spent fuel shipping cask. He basked in glory; nothing could touch him. If he stopped for an hour at a seedy hotel off the interstate, how would she know? It occurred to her that she never really knew for sure where her grown daughters were either. She recognized the depth of her ignorance. Daniel, whoever he was, did she even want him?

Faye opened her mouth as if in ecstasy, squinting through nearly closed eyes, and peed at last. When she was done, she pinched at the air. Iris let her up. Faye smiled at the high, filmy windows and screamed; the scream itself was nothing new. Maybe this was all there was to joy. Tears brimmed in Iris's eyes and fell down her cheeks. In the dayroom, Zdráv was reading a *Geographic* article on burn therapy. Iris thanked her and handed Faye over. The ward doors were opened to release her. The sun was too bright; it made her arms itch. She aimed for the dog Jack in the car.

At home she lit the stove and waited for Daniel to come home. The freezer vodka seemed to have lost its bite. Alcohol evaporated easily. She shouldn't have to explain that to Daniel. She drank the vodka, and the itch abated. For supper she heated leftovers: yesterday's duck, Tuesday's macaroni and cheese.

At eight-thirty Daniel parked his car in the garage, its tires steaming.

They sat down to supper. When she told him about visiting Faye, he nodded over the duck carcass as though he loved them both, her and her broken sister. She watched him swallow long strips of meat. "Stop looking at me," he said. "I can't eat with you looking at me."

She eyed him with sudden calm. Then she began her interrogation, speaking through her benumbed lips, although she saw that he was going to deny everything.

After a while he lost his good humor and banged on the table and jumped up. He raked his fingers angrily through his stiff hair. He said, "It's you. It's always been you." He went to watch TV.

"I'm not an idiot," Iris murmured under the drone of the dishwasher. She wasn't drunk enough yet, and she was out of vodka.

Daniel sat on the couch in the den, paring his fingernails over the coffee table. The clippers made little pinging sounds that made her wince. He caught at her hand as she passed by, and she pulled his fingers up to her mouth and bit them.

"Ow, ow!" was all he said. He took his coat from the back of the door. "I'm getting out of here," he told her. "I can take a hint. 'Get lost, Bub,' " he imitated what he thought she might say. Before he left, his eyes shifted down to her breasts and then away. Immediately she felt the other woman's irresistible skin growing there. What could she do? Ontogeny recapitulates phylogeny, Iris remembered from her high school days: a fetus sloughs the gill slits in its throat, the translucent domes over its eyes. She had come through the process once.

It's too late for that now, she thought.

Last Saturday: Daniel had mown the lawn, then slept all afternoon on the couch as if in penance, unmoving, his head against one bare wooden arm, his feet against the other. Twice she had gone in to wake him. When she leaned over him his eyes quivered beneath the lids, but did not open. The second time, she pulled off most of her clothes, and waited in her underwear. Daniel breathed and his flat chest rose under its motor oil stains. Abruptly his eyes snapped open and shut again, the mistake of a dream. He had not seen her.

Now she was rubbing petroleum jelly into her hands every night, and yet the new, red skin encroached from below. She felt herself to be highly flammable. She ran into the kitchen to see if she had turned off the stove.

For the rest of the evening she lay on the couch and watched old shows on television. A Mr. Magoo rerun was followed, logically, it seemed to her, by John Wayne in *Sands of Iwo Jima*. She thought about Wayne's remaining lung, and how like her he'd lost his gills—too bad. He was practically a dead man. He was going to die, and when he did, all the elements in his body would disperse. His molecules would probably be showing up in the bodies of other people, years from now, his carbon and ammonia and gold and whatnot. The thought of having to do it all over again made her ill. She searched for her car keys, wanting more vodka. Daniel must have taken them. She got a tube of lipstick from her purse and colored in her mouth. The slight, beaked shape of her lips was still her own. In her compact mirror, twisting, she examined the skin on her back. The other woman's skin was a faint membrane, from which she could never pick herself clean.

It was very late when the telephone rang. She sat up and held her aching head. When she answered, his voice washed toward her through the wires. She could not understand what he said. "Don't come home," she said into the petri dish of the receiver. She went out into the yard. In the moonlight his shirts and trousers took on postures of subjugation, and an idea came to her.

She found Daniel's army shovel in the garage and brought it out and started a hole. She dug at the end of the chain where Jack had been scratching. Pretty soon it was the size of a small foxhole, such as her beloved must have learned to dig in the army. Three foot by three and as deep, Iris figured. Nearby Jack lay with his long nose in his paws, guarding her.

She spat on her palms and wiped them on her jeans. This bad new skin dirtied easily. She put down the shovel and climbed out. She hauled Daniel's shirts and trousers from the line and threw them into the hole. "Liar," she said to Daniel, whose face she projected onto the clouds that floated behind the black trees. She gazed into the pit. His clothes looked good down there. For good measure she threw in Jack's stake, which took her a while to haul out because Daniel had embedded it in concrete, and last the bones of the Chinese duck. She shoveled the dirt in on top of them, burying the cuffed trousers, the oil-stained T-shirt of last Saturday. The limp arms of his shirts seemed to reach for her from the trench. She buried everything.

When she was done, she went back into the house and lit the stove. That was how Daniel found her fifteen minutes past midnight, holding her hands over the blue flames, slowly scorching her palms. She was practicing a recombinant sign. Her thoughts hissed like escaping oxygen. Get it? she sent to her rival. Feel me now? She would charbroil them both black as catfish if it would set her, Iris, free. She was howling like a banshee. The hypnotism wasn't working, but she felt better.

·   ·   ·

In the days and weeks following the burning of Iris's palms, it was Daniel who seemed the worse off for it. He looked at her recuperating in his recliner with her hands wrapped in neomycin and gauze, and all he could think of was what a dumb jerk he was. Was it too late for him/them? Some nights they argued it back and forth—by unspoken agreement, the nights without a baseball game or *The Waltons*. Sometimes a wash of calm would come over them. Iris could actually feel her own new skin growing then, as in a bath of agar; and Daniel rubbed his temples over and over to erase the thoughts he didn't want to be having. The two of them were the most separate they had ever been (except for before they'd met) and so in a way it was a good time. They stuffed themselves on cheap Salisbury steak TV dinners and supermarket beer. Some nights nothing disturbed them until, before they turned in, Iris had to ask Daniel to brush her teeth.

The last light on in the house was the one in the upstairs bathroom. Iris sat on a stool beside the sink, and Daniel maneuvered around her, brushing her crowns rigorously, while she looked up past his shoulder at the ceiling. It was a look that said, *I am already gone from you*. In that look, Iris took some degree of comfort.

"Rinse and spit," Daniel said, putting the cup of warm water to her lips. And she did so, holding her burnt hands up on either side of her in what might have been mistaken for a gesture of surrender. She was thinking of what was waiting for Ruth and Monica. Oh hell, Iris thought with rare clarity, as if you care how they are. Fuck the kids. They don't know what agony is yet. It was her element, and she was in it.

A History of Sex

I was working on a history of my body: a sex history, which hardly existed yet. I wanted to know why I was the way I was. Although people are not all the same, are they, so maybe I was all right. I took their test for the outside opinion.

"You don't equate sex with play," the teaching assistant said. The face test, the PIT, told him that. I'd volunteered myself as subject, one of two hundred sophomores on whom the TAs got to hone their interpretive skills. It was true that in my short life so far I found I liked sex alone, but not when it involved others; I could not stand to expose my want that way. I didn't mind watching. I liked to watch dogs when they fucked in the streets. But what aroused me, what I wanted a lover for, nobody else got to see that.

It was that way with me from the beginning. On

the grass outside the foreign languages building late one night, a Jesus follower let me ride him. He was an ex–tank driver out of Vietnam—we'd picked each other up in a bar only hours before. He lay on his back and opened his pants. He waited for me to lower myself; when I hesitated, he showed me his tongue. I had my choice. With his eyes on my face, with his wounded heart open, he waited. He had time.

I was seventeen then, a freshman, a recent migrant from home, and I wanted to arrive. He was trembling and grinning. Already I half wanted to smother him to keep him still. I made him close his eyes.

"Jesus, Ruth," he said. How could he know I'd never liked my name?

He was the first one I remember. I don't know how I knew what I knew, that sex was easier with strangers, or that I had to be the one on top. Even now, when I am under a lover, I stand no chance. Then he (or, more likely, she) watches me from a hundred miles up where the head floats in space—there I am, a dark country below. He thinks he has the map.

How could I know what I was? I hardly lived in my own body, although I'm not sure exactly when I realized this. One day in the hall shower I looked at myself. Without a mirror I couldn't see the important parts, namely head and back. What I did see, steaming breasts, the slight dome of the belly, the little inflator between the thighs, the dirty feet, this was my plastic blowup doll. It was not me. I knew it wasn't normal to think this way.

Close your eyes, I said to the Jesus man. But he saw me with his fingers.

There were no TVs allowed at the college. Aside from a battered black-and-white that turned up for Redskins games, there were none in the dormitory rooms or study lounges. A TV is a big help when you're looking back, trying to put things in proper order. How can I say for sure what happened on a given day if there were no news flashes, no official body count, to keep up with? I can't. The man I fucked in the grass wore dog tags stamped with his serial number. The face test was a onetime-only thing. The Friday that my father drove across two states to pull me out of college was a certain Friday on his calendar. But these events didn't show up on the picture tube. I saw vaguely that sex connected them, and not much else. The things that happened seemed to unhappen half the time. Every day I ate and slept and studied, from scratch to midnight. Then I had to get drunk all over again. What did I see when my eyes rolled back? I couldn't remember.

Only the unknowable stayed the same: my own face, which the mirror reversed; the white noise in my mind.

That first year I roamed the dormitory late at night, eating candy bars bought from the basement vending machines, not sure what I was doing there. Other girls seemed to know these things. They looked up at me incuriously from the green vinyl couches where they sat studying. They illuminated their textbooks with fluorescent highlighter. I went slow in the dark and used pencil. The monochromatic comforted me.

I thought I knew what separated me from them, Baptist girls in blood-red lipstick that came off on the backs of their hands quick enough when their daddies came visiting. I saw what sex meant to them, and how far they strayed from who they'd been raised to be. I went out drinking with those girls. I discovered I could outlast most of them, which boosted my confidence in that area, at least. By second term we were regulars in the local bars off campus. But I was still a virgin, and virginity was worthless. Nobody wanted their own.

The one who got mine was the Jesus man, the tanker. In the bar he was talking mechanics: the effect of mud on a tank's electrical system; the better speed, not to mention safety, you got with a diesel engine. His unit had covered ARVN's ass during the '71 Laotian operations, but that was all he would say about the actual war. You could tell he was talking to make himself real. Really, nobody cared. He was still alive and in one piece courtesy of his Savior, the skin dead white around his eyes, the blood permanently high in his cheeks. I asked him how he knew it was Jesus that saved him.

"Faith."

"Not the cast-steel armor. Not your cannons and machine guns."

"Believe or don't believe. Jesus loves you either way."

We went across the street and onto campus. In the moonlight in a sea of white grass he lay on his back, took my wrists, and pulled me down on top of him. I hadn't kissed much; but his tongue pacified and soothed me. He whispered to me about Jesus when I rode him. We did it at three in the morning, in public, sloshed to the point of oblivion—anyone passing could have watched if they'd wanted to. I wouldn't let him come inside me, so what we got was his salve all over everything. Afterward I felt hot and raw. I kept thinking of stray dogs I'd seen fucking. I felt as if I was one of them, my privates reddened like theirs. I could do it, then, behave in the flesh like anybody, like those dogs; so what? It wasn't making me happy or sad. He said I felt nice and tight inside.

Hours later I woke up alone in my bunk, with no memory of how I'd got there. I must have taken a shower; there was dried soap in my hair, the sheets were damp. On the floor beside me the immersion-heater coil was glowing in an empty cup. I marveled at the innocence of the dehydrated mind: boil water, make coffee. If there had been any, it was gone. It seemed best to cut my classes.

My roommate and I didn't get along, so by unspoken agreement we took turns with the room: she slept at her boyfriend's fraternity or I slept in the study lounge. When she stopped by that morning, she let me know I'd preempted her turn last night. It was comforting, the animosity I had toward her. I watched her trade one highlightered book for another. Her boyfriend, a ringer for her with his long pale hair and body (add a penis), lounged in the doorway. I caught him glancing at the bottle on my desk. I wasn't going to share my booze with them. It didn't matter what else I had stockpiled from the cafeteria, doughnuts or American cheese, I never offered them any. If I knew his name or he knew mine, I've forgotten. There were a thousand more like him outside that dorm, and plenty of ex-soldiers.

·　　·　　·

If I wanted to, the TA said, I could discuss my test results further with a college psychologist. He was serene behind his wire rims as he handed over the printout. He wanted me to know nothing fazed him. I knew what he thought. It was not true that I didn't like men. I had been with war veterans, not schoolboys; maybe in its perfection that test didn't allow for war. Besides, I loved my father.

When I was fourteen, fifteen, it was cool to sit beside my father in the den, lights out, watching the news on TV. He never touched me unless it was to drape his arm across my shoulders, and frankly, I was glad if he did. He was a restless type by any scale. What was home to him? It was us, he said, this family; you could pack it up and take it anywhere. In the sixties, when General Electric wanted to start up home-appliance production in Colombia, he had done just that. We were back in the U.S. now, in Carville. But a stalled moment with him still felt rare enough.

The Vietnam War transfixed him. Back then he followed the war, once it turned out to be a war, in a patriotic rage that he transformed by day into the business of refrigeration. Frequently he came home late from meetings with the R-and-D geniuses. They were designing a home deep freezer: it was going to be the average Joe's solution to skyrocketing meat prices.

People were buying red meat in bulk now, i.e., half a goddamn cow, and where could you stash a thing like that? His hair would be stiff; he needed a shower. We watched the news out of Vietnam at seven and eleven; we stuck it out until the broadcast credits rolled. We Mowrys were warmongers, hawks. My father had regrets over not seeing action in Korea, due to the bad eyesight that kept him stateside. I knew the depth of his shame without having to be told, same way I knew he loved me. My mother waited for him upstairs in her best nightgown, and he wouldn't go up until the body count had been pounded out on his knee.

He was all for carpet bombing the North, for invading Cambodia when it came to that in '70. When our black-and-white TV failed, he bought a color model. I was stunned by the gorgeousness of war in living color. My mother wouldn't watch the night he brought the new set home, saying no, it was awful, too lurid. "Blood isn't really that red," she said. "Look, I'll cut myself, I'll show you." We didn't move—we were used to her threats. She enjoyed making them. She was trying to put up with something she could not stand to put up with. She was getting an aura, which made her want total darkness, and Empirin compound against the migraine coming. She wanted me to sit with her upstairs, but I wouldn't do it. Monica, my younger sister, was roped into that job. Monica, so good with doll bodies, made the switch to our mother easier than I would have.

The sight of carnage didn't seem to bother my father much. He was a good father to me.

The next was another veteran, U.S. Army Signal Corps. I wasn't looking for soldiers, but the college was near Forts Eustis and Stacy. They came into the bars starved for a kind of human companionship they could no longer bear. They had borne it before, so easily. And now women made them curl and shiver. They trusted only each other. They slunk in and out of your room hardly looking at you over their shoulders, and you understood it because you were the same way. You were leery of gentleness, you shied from easy reach. Why was that? You can't know the sense of some things. (Maybe I was born leery. I used to cry at the rabbit shadows my father's hands made on the wall. I thought his fingers had eyes.)

I brought the signalman up to my room. I had planned to follow certain rules—not to know their names, not to bring them home—but I let him come up. It was a warm night, and the humid air brought on heat lightning and palmetto bugs. What we did felt dangerous, and all it was was words.

Later his face wouldn't come to me. I was left with

the sound of his dull voice speaking, not sweet Jesus words like the tanker, but porn. *Cunt* (he must have said it, else where'd I get the idea?), *hole*, *slit*. I was familiar with the Eat Meat poster, its butcher's map dividing a woman's body into flank and loin. We were very drunk. Cunt, he said, more a grunt than a word; and I was stupid, splayed on the bed. He kept bumping my thigh, frantic for the hole between my legs. *Where is it?* I wasn't wet yet, but I showed him and, still stupid, got banged raw. This was sex when I was willing, when the man I brought to my room was not so sick as to smother me. Afterward we lay breathing the acetic smells of bug dirt, sex, and ozone.

I think now, maybe I could have fallen in love with girls. I wasn't going to figure that out for a while. Girls didn't do girls.

I knew I didn't want love from men. Their words in my head weren't pleasant. I did not want to end up like my mother, tricked by static in the phone lines— your señoritas are back, she'd say to my father. Meaning the women my father knew while he was stationed at White Sands, decades ago. He said he was a virgin when he married her, and she said she believed him; this was their official history. On the other hand, she claimed the Mexicans still pestered her with their silky voices. Maybe this just got her left alone from our end, maybe some real peace and quiet.

I wasn't sleeping much. Time went by unevenly: I couldn't make five minutes stick, but a whole day was a mire. I missed a lot of morning classes, although the men I had sex with didn't stay over and I didn't want them to. A black seaman from Norfolk taught me the lotus position. I might remember positions, or parts of their bodies, but never faces.

Every so often there would be a test in one subject or another. In some I didn't progress. During my second year I had to repeat Physics 101: I understood Newton's laws of motion well enough, but not much else. In philosophy there were long harangues on whether God existed (unprovable; he eluded us), whether time travel might someday be possible (sadly, no). I gave up the idea of majoring in history, the quantum physics of fact and antifact. We'd had our turn in Vietnam, after the Chinese and the Japanese and the French; now we turned tail and ran. Everybody knew it; worse, some people lied and said they knew all along the U.S. couldn't win and ought to get out. I wasn't so hawkish anymore, but I didn't deny that I had been. I didn't understand this thing I had for soldiers. By the spring of my sophomore year I had been with half a dozen others, warm breathers all. None of them had touched me.

.   .   .

In the late twentieth century we fortunates had the faces on the PIT to explain us to ourselves. This was how it was put to us on the flyers sent under our doors. Two hundred–odd sophomores showed up on a Saturday to take the Picture Identification Test—the face test. Sweating in our jungle-green ponchos, we waited in the rain for the psychology building doors to open. Whoever I'd been with the night before had not been gentle, but then I liked that, although now there were marks.

The test was given in a lecture hall below the labs. A massive green chalkboard spanned the wall behind the lecturer's stone table; on another wall the periodic table listed the 105 known elements, each one complete in itself. The curved rows of seats rose up and up. The proctors sat us as for a final, with empty seats between us. Why? We couldn't cheat. In psychology the obvious answer is often the wrong one.

I was feeling all right that day. Things were bothering me less than usual. The proctors handed out free pencils, good ones, Mongol No. 2s. The test itself was nothing but black-and-white photographs of people. What drew you in was that each person was shown making a series of faces, like the ones you'd make in a coin-op photo booth, but for scientific purposes. For each person there were questions: which face transmits rage, which I'm a fool for love, etc. To study the faces was fascinating and disturbing; it was like looking into a series of mirrors in which you were not yourself. It was page after page of you—except your features kept changing, your supposed private feelings were on public display. Around me the other students were bent-necked over their tests. The test booklets varied at random (again to foil cheaters); were some faces more pliant, more revealing? Mine showed mostly rage and desire. Love seemed invisible. I was not allowed to know their thoughts, so I tried to guess at what provoked them. What made this man smile? What froze his girlish twin? But you don't have to know, I told myself, blackening the answer circles. The lecture hall was still except for occasional coughing and the scratch of pencils, and the blinking black-and-white codes of our answers, which were going to be fed into the department's massive computer for analysis.

Nothing tangible existed between any two faces: no eyes met; no one's fingers ran through another's hair; nobody kissed. The test faces came without histories. I thought, That's nothing new. Sirhan Sirhan on our television at home, how motionless his face had been, how we could read nothing there, and we said, *Well, he's an Arab, a foreigner.* We were illiterate in foreign faces. And we were just as dumb with our own: Oswald, Ruby, even James Earl Ray looked the same to us, all those killers did. A face told you nothing. At his drunkest, my father's face was a blank.

The proctors called time. We passed our tests toward the aisles. Outside it was still raining, so people milled around in the hall, eating the free doughnuts and laughing too loud. I left. I didn't know any of them, and they didn't know me.

That night I went down to the dorm basement and hung around the vending machines. The study lounge was empty, the girls I drank with were out on actual dates. I wanted to tell somebody about the face test. But what could I say? I felt nervous and lonely; I wasn't sure anymore why I had volunteered or what I'd revealed. I sat in the pay phone booth with the door closed and ate a candy bar. I might have called my father, but it was so late, after midnight he was asleep in bed beside my mother.

When I tried to make myself come, first in that cramped wooden booth and later on my bunk, nothing worked. My body wouldn't respond. Unless I was sloshed I couldn't stand the idea of anybody watching me; and I felt watched, as if the faces were paying me back. At the same time it was no comfort finding out how anonymous a person really was. So I wouldn't give up trying. I did shots of tequila and fingered my softer parts in a haze until I went to sleep.

I translated for myself what the TA said. The body's got no equator. Looking around in the dark for the place where you began? You need to relax, baby. It was there in his face.

So I took the option. The counseling offices were in the same building that the test had been given in, top floor. I checked the frosted-glass doors along the corridor until I found one with my assigned shrink's name cut into it. I guessed he still had faith in a cold, hard fact. Otherwise Dr. Joseph Deal was almost one of us in his ponytail and sandals. "Call me Joe," he said.

He spread open the fanfold paper and read my test scores. I'd ranked the need for defendance highest, followed by achievement and, weirdly, abasement. I thought we might get into that last one. He said we could, but then he read the sex part. What most people associated positively, I'd associated negatively. You have not learned, it said, that you play best when you are free and uninhibited. "It doesn't sound like you're having much fun."

I wasn't? Of course not.

He was giving me the go-ahead look. Stock-in-trade, I thought, watching him back. Was he for real?

"What do you think? Talk to me, Ruth Mowry. Why be passive."

It was getting harder to fake it, Joe Deal, that's what I wanted to say. I was sitting on his couch as far away from him as I could get. I knew what I looked like, and he was a man. Sunglasses left the skin around my eyes white; my hair was uncombed, my fingers nicotined. Here, where I would never allow it, I wanted to cry.

I wasn't saying much, so Deal talked for a while. The test was just a diagnostic tool; all it could do was point us in the right direction. He said it was apparent that something was wrong, something manifesting as an anesthetized affect and a lack of sexual pleasure. He said if we talked about it, things might go better. I remember that word *pleasure* sawing at me, how bad it made me feel.

"Sex isn't play," I said.

"What do you think it is?"

"It's the same as hunger. Which is fine with me."

"Come on. You're nineteen, you know what goes on. Most kids your age think sex is almost as much fun as acid."

"I don't trip."

"Ah—Republican?"

"Not really." It bothered me that his own face gave away no category of affect that I could see. Why was it okay for his face to be like that? I didn't feel like bantering.

He drew his red leather chair closer. I had to get out of there. He said, "Because it's in our national manifesto: you have the right to pursue happiness. That's why we're here."

"I like sex okay."

"You like it okay."

He was pissing me off. "What do you want me to say, it's a real blast, it's the damn neutron bomb? I can do it, if that's what you mean."

"Actually, you're just getting started. Women don't reach sexual prime until thirty, thirty-five." He grinned. "Am I making you uncomfortable?"

I wasn't going another round. "Fuck this."

"It's good, anger. It's telling us you know you're missing out on something."

I made the next appointment, but I didn't think I was going back. I was not now, nor had I ever been, *passive*. Why were they all on me? My sexual parts worked. I had proved it. I had lubricated and heaved and come. As long as the body works, who cares how one feels about it? That was how I felt.

There was no one session that broke me, and none that fixed me later on. Deal said, We'll get to the bottom of this. But there was no bottom—I was not a box. One evening I shouted at him: I *had* a box all right but I *was not* a box! He was taken aback by my vehemence. He relit his pipe, jiggling his foot while he considered me. He said he was worried about me. He said *he* didn't matter; only what he and I did here mattered. The fan was noisy. I lost some of his words.

I think it was Deal who called my parents.

My father drove across the states of Tennessee and Virginia to get me. Maybe it wasn't Deal. Other circumstances might have led to my father's coming. For instance, I was failing Latin American history and physics again. He would have known about that. I don't see how he could have known that I was sleeping in my clothes. Or that, when my cigarettes ran out, I stole butts from the study lounge ashtrays. It was a benign form of sex to me, to put my lips where other lips had been. It could make me breathe a little rougher. Maybe somebody saw me.

He called my dorm one afternoon from a motel just off campus—out of the blue, he was that close. "You've got us worried half to death," he said. "I've come to take you home." It wasn't much warning, I said, and hung up. I had somehow forgotten that I had a father, whose money still fed and clothed and housed me. When he walked in ten minutes later, I was in my underwear having a cigarette. His face flushed and he went to throw open the window. "Don't," I said. It was a thrill to see him hesitate at the sound in my voice. As if by rote I put on blood-red lipstick and a sleeveless dress. I told him I was hungry so we could get out of there.

He had rented a big tank of a car, a yellow Delta 88 with black interior. I admired its gas capacity. I slammed the door when I got in. My father flinched but said nothing. I could see he cared about this car even though in a few hours it'd be out of his hands, and it didn't matter to him what atrocities had ever happened on that flat backseat. Finally he said Bruno Hauptmann's widow was yapping about Bruno's innocence again. Imagine that. He was still upset over the kidnapping of the Lindbergh baby, after forty years.

I took him to the Chinese restaurant, which in tidewater Virginia in 1974 was a rarity, albeit the suspect kind. My father ran his hand along the black lacquer bar and marveled at the bordello-red walls and booths and the starched white tablecloths with Chinese characters stamped on the underside by the laundry. "Fabulous!" he said. On the little TV that hung above the bar, a Buddhist monk was burning. It was file footage, already familiar (that was the horror, if I'd thought about it). For perhaps the twentieth time I watched the fire engulf him, and again, he held still. Was this the act of a passive man? I didn't think so.

My father was a hawk, and what was I? I had my doubts; by degrees I was turning dovish, and anyway the U.S. was almost out of it. But I missed the war. I wanted to believe in a surgical strike that could separate good from evil. I coveted the armor that seemed alive on the ground, the APCs, the creeping tanks; I appreciated the Huey's bird's-eye view of the armies of deliverance. Although as we all know it turned out there was no deliverance; nobody went free. I feel a ration of shame now for my wrongful views on that war, but I didn't then.

"Strange stuff," my father said, when we were settled in a booth over plates of foo yung.

"You'll like it," I said. "It's got egg in it."

"You know me pretty good."

I said I still doused eggs with maple syrup as he'd taught me, which pleased him. Maybe he had come for these bits of language, the one he and I spoke, the one my mother asked to be left out of. "Leave me out of it," she'd say at her most acquiescent; other times she said much worse. She said she had enough nonsense coming at her through the phone lines—meaning the señoritas. She was distracted and had a hard time coming back to us.

"She thinks I'm having an affair," my father said.

But she had always thought so.

"Are you?"

He finished the rice in his cheek, glaring. Then he barked, "What? What?"

"You brought it up, Dad." I was trying to think. Did a fork have enough edge to cut foo yung? Everything the Chinese eat is manageable with sticks, only I kept losing hold. I must be scared, I thought. I knew I couldn't let him pull me out of there.

My father regarded me. The booth was narrow and I felt him breathing me in with the air. Nothing much was wrong between us, and yet it was throwing me to be alone with him like this, having a private dinner in a nearly empty restaurant under the eyes of waiters, my father buying me drinks—"Have what you like," he said, finally, and for himself ordered another vodka with lime. "What rot are they filling your head with here, anyway? Why study English? You already speak it." This was kind of him to say. My father was not as hard on me as my mother was, but neither of them wanted stupid children. Under the table he patted my knee. He was forgiving me.

"It's physics. I'm failing physics."

"I'll come right to it," he said. "I came all this way to see for myself, since you won't talk to us on the phone. Are you on drugs?"

I told the truth, but it felt like a lie. "No."

"Swear to me."

"E pluribus unum."

He said he wasn't joking. He said he knew I was sleeping in my clothes, and that I'd been warned about scrounging in the cafeteria Dumpsters. I asked him who'd ratted on me, how he knew.

"I got a call."

"From who?"

"It doesn't matter."

"Matters to me," I said angrily.

"Ruthie," he said. Sleeplessness had heightened my senses; I could smell the Vitalis in his hair, the leather slide-rule case in his shirt pocket. "Let me take you home. You decide you want to be a rocket scientist, you can always finish later. Don't worry, I'll still pay."

I didn't need to go home. If I wanted to I could set myself on fire, now I'd seen how it was done. Why was his goddamn hand on my knee? I wasn't talking yet. Five fingers and a palm, that's all a hand was. A soldier told me he had seen hands in the trees in Vietnam. Picture it: A man steps on a mine, what parts are going to catch? His trigger finger, his wedding ring. Like birds they were in the trees, the soldier said. Common as parrots. He'd yawned to show me how common they were. I didn't mention this to my father.

"I need Joe more than I need you," I said.

"That headshrinker?"

"Any headshrinker."

138

That got to him. In spite of the fans he was sweating, radiating heat. He mopped his forehead with the red napkin; real linen, it had come folded into a lotus shape. "I don't get it. I'm your father, nobody wants your happiness more than me." It was quite a lot for him to say. "Does this Joe make you happy?"

"It doesn't work like that."

"How does it work, then? Tell me."

I shook my head. You don't get to know, I thought. The tongue with which I had eaten was curling in my mouth. The egg foo yung sat in its serving dish, going jelly cold under the brown gravy.

After a while he said he had paid for a room with two double beds in it, in case I wanted a good night's sleep before I rode back home with him, as he still hoped I would. "Wouldn't you like that?" he asked. "A double bed instead of an iron bunk, for a change? A hot shower, color TV? You don't have to decide immediately, I'm not leaving till morning. Your mother misses you. Even your sister misses you."

Monica was a rabbity little thief, but I didn't tell him that. She was the model teenager, invisible. She didn't need me to help her keep out of sight. I hoped she was happy, not that any of us would ever know.

"Don't ask me anymore," I said.

Out on the sidewalk, a stray was licking itself. A huge gray dog, collarless, breed unknown. We had to pass it on the way to the car. Its fat red penis was fully extended out of the sheath. It was impossible to tell if there was any pleasure to the licking or only hygiene. My father, brooding, would not be distracted. He lowered his head and pretended not to see what the dog was doing.

I quit the march and stopped to stare at the dog. The drinks I'd had were making my head roar, but I knew what I was doing. I was ambushing my father, waiting for him to turn around. I was thinking, You are not the only one, Dad. I don't have to go anywhere with you. Why had it taken so long to know this? I watched every deviation the dog's tongue took, every quiver the red flesh made.

My father was ahead several feet before he realized. "Ruth! Come on."

I looked up to see him flush. I stood in the road and caught the old ache live on his face. It was fun, it gave me a kick, it was pure pleasure to see it there.

"Goddamn it, come on!"

"Why?" I said. "Am I bothering you?" I stayed where I was. The dog went on nosing itself and licking; a dog has no shame. My father got into the car and closed the door, cutting me from his sight. I think he knew then he'd lost me.

.   .   .

What makes you think it ends? It never ends. Girls still grow up like me. I wanted to be able to beg for what I wanted without shame.

I would have slept with a VC if I could have found one. Instead I went to bed with one of the Chinese waiters from the restaurant. He was from Taiwan and not the Communist mainland, but my father recognized no such distinctions, and neither did most Vietnamese. I courted the irony in my sleeping with our mutual and historic enemy. He was as close as I could get to what I needed. He was our waiter that night; and I had seen him, on other nights, doing his Chinese exercises in the parking lot. Stocky, his glasses winking in the street lamp, he had a steady kind of grace. There was no stopwatch on him; time just ran on. His eyes did not see me, but he knew I was there. He spoke little English. We took an empirical approach. I felt no more shame over my sex acts with him than I would have over verbal conversation. He was smooth skinned, a good lover, though his hands smelled of peanut oil.

"The running-dog lackeys are leaving now," the barman had murmured after my father, in Chinese, but we understood him.

I went back at closing time, after my father had gone to his motel up the road. I followed the Chinese waiter upstairs to his haven above the restaurant, a narrow room with a futon in it and a radio on the floor alongside. I went to bed with him, although I did not know him. While we were doing it, I kept watch on my father. He was with me—not in the flesh (sick idea), but in my mind he was as close as that radio. The Chinese man and I were kissing, and my father passed his hand across his eyes, as though he were very tired and would like to lie down. We were stripping off our shirts, and the Chinese man licked my nipples to harden them, while my father spoke on the telephone to my mother, some four hundred miles away; and I said to my foreign lover, Do you love me? which he did not understand. It was just a joke I thought up, as my mother listened jealously at the kitchen receiver and my father fixed himself another drink. The gray dog cleaned its red penis: Was it ready yet? Was I? The Chinese man was preparing his hands, washing and drying them, rubbing in oils for suppleness and vitality, rubbing them for me. The whisk of his palms had a sound like quick breathing. I lay on my stomach on the open futon, and he straddled me and massaged my shoulders. From underneath him, I saw my father as he appeared in the motel mirror: his face was swollen and exhausted; he could not see straight. He picked up his razor and tested the blade. He wanted me to look through his eyes for him, but I wouldn't do it.

I felt the Chinese man enter me from behind. I felt

his slow strokes, his smooth chest pressing against my back. I felt myself come open. I hardly ever came open; it felt good. I could smell our mingled smells, oil and rusty blood. We were in no hurry. Neither was my father across town, who would probably nick himself and need a styptic, and when the vodka was gone he'd drive the half mile to the package store, where another bottle waited for him faithful as a woman, as almost any woman.

In the morning when I woke up, I was in the Chinese man's arms, as near to safe as any baby. We were lying on the futon, and he was still asleep. Through the window I could see stark white rags on the kitchen roof's clothesline. I could hear the ROTC drilling on the quad, firing blanks that reported against the buildings. The girl had knelt openmouthed at Kent State four years before; I expected she'd gotten up again by now.

I got up and found a cloth and washed my face and hands in the sink. I put warm water in a bowl and brought it to the bed. He was awake now; he was watching me. I pulled back the sheet and, gently, I washed him. I washed his soft penis, cradling him in my palm while I made the water run over its velvet, its blind mouth. I washed the thirsty soles of his feet. He smiled at me with a stranger's tenderness. "Baby doll," he said haltingly. Then we told each other our real names.

.   .   .

That spring the nation saw the last of campus rallies against the bombing of Indochina. Certain crises at home superseded the war. We were onto Nixon himself now. Watergate never seemed to end; brawls over school busing made the news on local TV. I did go home for the Fourth of July, but that was all. A lot of people were calling for Nixon's impeachment. My mother, ever the loyalist, remained convinced of his innocence. Wait, she argued with the TV, wait a minute, it's not all black-and-white. Was she talking about some other Nixon? Even his dog was black-and-white—Checkers. But, true, he was a bloody man underneath.

I had to find a way through the world. There was money in my father's pockets, and he sent me some. The Chinese say the only thing you can buy with money is want, and more want; but my Chinese lover gave me what he could. I had shelter, clothing, and take-out food. I had my sex history written out on graph paper, and when I looked down in the shower I saw my own feet holding me up. The TV in the Chinese restaurant went on the fritz, so no war news came in from any front, foreign or domestic. I was glad. Hardly any war was nice for a while.

Dogfight

On Thursday Carl brought home the brindle dog. Monica looked up from the red couch where she sat reading and saw him standing in the kitchen doorway with the brindle on a dirty rope. Carl shrugged and untied the rope. The dog eyed her from back of Carl's legs. "Here," she said to it. "Here, boy." She crooned low in her throat and held out her hand.

"He's scared," Carl said, poking the dog.

The dog went to Monica on shaking legs. He was narrow and ribby and she could see he had greyhound in him. There were cuts in his hide. He wasn't a good-looking dog. For Carl's sake, she wanted to like him more than she did. "What hole did you crawl out of?" she said to the dog. When she touched his ears he flinched and growled, and she turned her hand in the air, showing him emptiness.

"I bought him off Troutman," Carl said. "He was hanging around Troutman's runs. The guy was going to shoot him, today or tomorrow."

Troutman raised cocker spaniels in the house behind their house. One or another of his bitches was always in heat. His radio was playing faintly through the trees outside; he kept it on all the time, claimed it soothed his cockers. A stray dog was a weasel to Troutman.

"He made you pay?"

"Troutman for you," Carl said. He curled his fingers into the shape of a pistol. "I gave him ten."

The brindle had quit smelling her hand. She let him nose between her legs for a second, knowing he needed to. Then she pushed the dog away.

Carl took off his cap and ran his fingers through his cut-back yellow hair. He washed his hands in the kitchen sink. "I'll put him out with Fred."

"Fred won't like it," Monica said. No dogs ever hung around their own run, since Fred, her old brown dog, was the only one in it.

"It might work," Carl said.

When he came back in she said, "So?"

"Everything went fine."

They ate supper without speaking much. Carl didn't like to eat and talk at the same time. Monica

watched him wipe his lips on his napkin. She thought,
He is going to be so happy in a minute.

After the dishes were cleared, Monica took out the
pregnancy test kit from the drugstore. She had already
performed the test. "This line means I did it right,"
she said. "You can't really do it wrong." She showed
him the blood-red indicator inside the circle. She
watched him, zeroing in on his face so she could spot
when that bursting-open moment of joy hit him, but
somehow she missed it. Maybe it was too hard to see.

"That's it?" Carl said in disbelief.

Carl used to bet the greyhounds over in Pensacola,
until Monica put a stop to that. It was in his nature to
want some announcer to tell him what he was seeing
with his own two eyes. Now, he stared at the little
paper circle. "I think I liked it better when a rabbit
died." He laughed nervously.

"No, wait—" She showed him the second line. It
was a faint trace, but it was there. "That's the real one."

He leaned across the table and kissed her. Then he
laid his flat hand on her forehead. She caught a whiff
of fertilizer. She'd been smelling that smell on him
since they'd met in dirt class at Florida State Ag and
Tech; even so, she had to jump up for some reason.
She milled around in the kitchen, dropping plates into
the sink water.

"I don't have a fever. It isn't like that," she said, irritated.

Carl gazed at her. Tears came out of his eyes in a slow course, and he smiled.

She heard the new dog bleat in the run, and the other dog, Fred, give his odd quavery bark. "They're getting along," she told Carl. She went back toward him and petted his bristly yellow-white hair, and he relaxed against her, his ear to her belly.

They drove out the next afternoon to the trailer park off 90, east of Pensacola, where Monica's father was staying. Her father was burning vines when they arrived. He said they were poison-ivy vines. Monica could tell her father was already tight.

Carl said, "They better not be poison-ivy vines." All of them had breathed the smoke by now.

"It's a joke," Monica's father said. "Trying to get a rise out of her." He jerked his thumb at Monica. "Want a beer, help yourself, Carl."

He fried cheese sandwiches on white bread for them on his sterno stove under the awning. He had learned to cook since his retirement. He used to be chief engineer of G.E.'s refrigeration division; with eleven patents, he was the expert of cold. Occasionally he'd mention how it got under his skin that, legally, his ideas were company property.

"What's the big deal about cooking?" he said. "It's simple thermodynamics." Monica watched him cut papery slices of cheese with his jackknife. One of the other trailers had a backed-up sewage line, which they could smell as they ate. Her father offered Carl a beer, and Carl took it. Carl sighed at the way she was eyeing the both of them, and said it was all right.

"Oh, fine, then," Monica said with some annoyance. She knew when she had been deserted. "You have to make it easier for him?"

"Come on, the man's still on his feet."

"I can't quite remember why we had you," her father said, gazing at the tops of the cottonwoods. Then he turned and tipped his glass at her as if he were offering her respect.

Monica's father was drinking lime rickeys, made with vodka instead of gin. It was a drink he had learned to drink in nightclubs, after the Korean War, which he hadn't been to because his eyes were bad. Monica remembered him drinking this drink from her childhood. In spite of everything she liked the name, *rickey*. She thought of how, once, he had let her watch while their doctor cut a slow-growing mole from his side. Him up on the examining table in a jokey mood, bantering: "Hey, Doc! A tumor grows same as a baby, am I right?" The doctor handed her a vial of smelling salts, although she was fifteen and perfectly lucid and unafraid. Now she was having a delayed reaction. Her father and Carl were talking in buzzing voices, and she was thinking about yellow belly fat. Grudgingly, she lifted the lid of the cooler and helped herself to a beer. "Have you heard from Mom?" Monica said, when she hadn't said anything for a while.

Her father turned on the radio and jiggled the tuner. "Her life is too good now. That new guy she's with is taking her to Acapulco, she hasn't got time for me." The radio announcer gave the time. Monica's father cut back a laugh. "She wants to dive off some hundred-foot cliff. I hope she cracks her skull."

The vine pile had nearly burned down. There were little crackles from it every so often. Carl tried to tell her father about the new dog. "He looks fast. I bet I can teach him to course a lure." But Monica's father wasn't particularly interested.

After lunch her father started playing around, nudging Carl in the ribs. Monica wished she hadn't brought up her mother. "Ever pay for it?" her father said, patting his belly where the grilled cheese had gone. "Guy like you, had to pay yet?"

Monica shot Carl a look, but Carl wouldn't agree to leave that minute.

"Yeah," Carl said, answering her father's question. "But not lately." He ducked his head and winked at Monica, trying to kid her along. It wasn't going to work.

"Let the buyer beware, though, huh," Monica's father said languidly. "You get what you pay for. Luckily I still have plenty of money."

"Hey, should we tell him?" Carl asked her, to change the topic.

"What? What?" Monica's father had a crust of sugar from the lime rickey on his upper lip.

"You have sugar on you, Dad," Monica said. She pictured her father's swollen fingers clutching a woman's breast as if it were a stone he could throw, a defensive gesture made in fear rather than desire. Had he clutched her mother that way, too, or just some whore? She eyed Carl with glinty eyes. Dad's disgusting, she thought, both of them are. But she leaned over and brushed the sugar from her father's lip with her pinkie. His skin was looser on him than she remembered. "Mom shouldn't have left you."

"Damn right," her father said. "I took her to Tampa Bay for the ASME conference. She learned to water-ski because of me."

Carl and Monica waited by the rear wheels of the trailer while her father rolled up last night's steak bone in a piece of newspaper for Fred. There was just the one bone. Her father gave it to her and then he took her by the shoulders. "Night-night," he said. The aluminum trailer had turned blue in the twilight. He kissed her cheek with his rimy mouth. His lips stuck a little.

"Carl," Monica said in her clear voice. "Carl."

In the truck she felt the grease from the bone cut through the newspaper and soak her jeans. Now it's two dogs, she thought. She wanted to yell at Carl. She threw the bone out the truck's window. There was nothing to accuse him of. She had no real suspicions. Not lately, he'd said, which meant *before you*. She could smell the tree fertilizer on him; it was in his sweat. When he patted her leg, she pushed him away. "Don't." She put her hands up under her shirt and felt her hot belly.

When they fought at home later, Monica tried to hit Carl, but he caught her arm and held it high above both their heads. She looked sorry until he let her go. Then she hammered herself in the head with her fists, screaming at him, "Pay me, then! Pay me!"

Carl backed up. "That's enough, Monica," he said. He threw his hands up at her and walked away. Neither of them said anything more about it.

She heard the dogs gurgling low in their throats at each other, out in the run.

·   ·   ·

The sound of one of the dogs throwing itself against the wire fence Monday morning made Monica get up from the couch. Carl had left for work already. She looked out the kitchen window. The brindle was hurling himself at the locked gate, coming from way back in the run. When he leapt, the fence gave, and then sprang back, tossing him off. She watched the brindle land heavily on the ground, his claws scratching as he righted himself. She could see Fred lying on his side in the cool mud.

The next time the brindle came down, he startled Fred by landing on him. Through the glass Monica saw Fred jump up snarling. Still, Fred blinked; the brindle seized the older dog by the neck, as if he might tear his way free; through wire or flesh, it made no difference.

When she got there with the length of pipe in her hand, though, Fred was leaning back on his haunches, his tongue lathered, and it was Carl's dog gurgling in the bright mud. She couldn't picture what had happened to reverse their order, but there was the brindle dying in front of her. His speckled side heaved and his blood gushed from the main in his throat and he died. Carl is going to be upset, she thought. Am I inhuman? She couldn't seem to feel anything. It was a problem she had sometimes, although it didn't always feel like one. She had to depend on herself during emergencies.

She dragged the pipe along the wire to keep Fred back as she opened the gate. It was a gesture; she saw that the old brown dog would not attack her. His hot breath wavered at her shoulder as she knelt. She unbuttoned her shirt and wrapped the brindle's throat with it, knowing it was too late for that. His eyes were glassy. She could hear voices from Troutman's radio coming through the trees. Monica shivered in her bra. A light steam was coming off the body. She felt watched; she thought, Well how do people know dogs don't have souls? The brindle's was hovering over her in the morning air. Fred stood by, bleeding patiently from the side of his neck.

Monica rearranged the shirt as a ground cloth under the dead dog. She dragged the body out of the run and up the slope toward the house. She imagined him following her through the air, mean and scared because he couldn't feel earth under him, so she tried not to hurt him; though it was ridiculous, she pulled as gently as she could. She left his body in the grass beside the garage drainpipe. Then she went back for Fred.

Inside the run the ground was torn and ruined. Wasps were coming from a pile of tires back in the trees between the houses. She crouched and examined the brown dog. "Fred," she said. "Damn it, Fred." Fred's eye rolled back to watch her hands. The bite to his neck had missed the artery. She took him by the collar and led him toward the garage, giving the drain-pipe a wide berth. He was covered with mud, which stanched the bleeding somewhat. In spite of this her hands turned red and slippery. In the garage she took down a tarp that Carl kept for trips in bad weather. Fred lay on his side for her, and she cleaned him up best she could, and used half a tube of neomycin on the wound. Fred was all worn out. His caked fur smelled like almonds. She rubbed his nose for him and let him whine.

When Carl came home he pulled the truck up short in the garage. He came into the house. Monica was sitting on the red couch. "What's with Fred?" Carl said. He slapped his hands on his pants to get the chalky fertilizer off them. He ran his scraped, tarry hands under hot water in the sink. "I brought supper," he said. "Hardee's all right?"

Monica didn't want to tell him. She didn't answer. Troutman's radio was keeping those cockers quiet. At the sink Carl peered out the kitchen window. There was a pause, and Monica knew he was looking all around the run, as if the brindle might have had any-place to hide out there. "Where's my dog?" Carl said.

"He's out by the drainpipe. I saved him for you."
She met his stare in the best way she could. She
wanted to plead, but he was against her dog already.
"He bit Fred, and Fred had to kill him."

"What?" Carl said.

She said nothing.

"He's dead?"

"Fred couldn't help it."

Carl kept washing his hands, grabbing at his fingers as if they were strange to him. Then he shook off
the dirty fertilizer water and went out to the garage.
She was afraid for Fred, but she didn't follow him. In a
little while Carl came back inside. His boots made
marks on the kitchen floor. His hands were stained
red. He didn't wash them again. Silently she cleaned
the marks.

They ate slowly, side by side at the kitchen table,
their jaws working. They ate the take-out that Carl
had brought home. They ate french fries with cold
ketchup and burgers with yellow cheese on top. The
meat was brown, gray on the inside, but even cold
it tasted good to her. Then, gradually, she began
to hear Fred whining in the garage. He was weak,
and the hollow garage door was made of metal.
She knew that Carl heard him too, but he just reached
for pie.

They peeled open the square boxes marked "Apple" and ate the pie inside. Carl asked for a glass of lemonade. She wasn't expecting him to want lemonade. When he said he wanted it, Monica got up and took a frozen can from the freezer. The waxy tube of the can soothed her hot hands. While she was making the lemonade she found a smear of blood on her forearm. She had her back to Carl. She put her arm under the tap and watched the blood run off into the pitcher, where it plumed and disappeared. It was nothing he had to see, she thought; it was surprising how much it looked like blood in a toilet. Unexpectedly she felt low, even angry. Should Fred have let himself be torn apart? He was a good dog; he wasn't one that liked fighting. She stirred the lemonade and watched Carl drink it. Then she cleared away the plates.

After supper she sat with Fred on the garage floor. Carl came and stood over her. His face looked bleached under the harsh overhead light, his scalp showing through his cropped hair. She could not bring herself to move. Fred was breathing heavily, his short ribs rising and falling as she stroked his crisp, small ears. "Are you coming to bed?" Carl said in a voice that was almost normal.

Fred twitched and growled as if he was having a dream.

"He's hurt," Monica said. "I'll be in soon."

Carl turned and went into the house without a word.

Later, when she led Fred back to the run, she saw Carl. He was standing, shirtless, in front of the plate-glass window in the den, his arms spread out flat as if he were attaching himself to the glass. She saw the tubercles of his eyes and nipples. As she looked he dropped his arms and faded back into the house.

She opened the run gate. Fred lay down in the mud. She thought, Well, it wasn't mud that hurt him. She listened to his slow, gusty breathing. The whites of his eyes showed dull as coral.

Inside the house, waves of darkness. She bolted shut the garage door by feel. The kitchen wall seemed to buckle slightly as she touched it. She opened the refrigerator door, and the light went on, and she saw her own hand reaching in. It was many fingered and stained with mud. Her father had taught her the mechanics of its motions: applying force through the fingers' lever bones, you pinch and grasp. She lifted out a quart of milk. She pinched open the lip and filled her mouth with cold, thin milk, swallowing repeatedly. Only she couldn't get enough of it, so she set the quart down again on the wire rack. The light was leaking over everything. She closed the door. Its form dissolved before her eyes, the particles of light scattering.

Gradually she made out the oily window and the curve of the white sink below. She moved toward the back of the narrow house to the bedroom.

Carl was not asleep. He was watching TV in the dark with the sound off, a pillow stuffed under his head. Monica got undressed, taking off her work boots and jeans and underwear. She took Carl's T-shirt from the back of the chair and put it on. She lay down beside him, the shirt twisting around her ribs. Carl rose on one elbow and rolled toward her. His face loomed. She put her hand out and felt the shape of his mouth as if she were blind. "I know you loved that dog, Carl," she said.

His teeth gleamed in the flickering light. "I thought I was saving him," he said. "Isn't that dumb of me."

She went to stroke his head and he wiped his damp eyes roughly on the sheet. His leg crossed over hers. She felt his penis harden against her thigh. He took her wrists and held her to the bed. He was climbing her, and she said, "Carl, I'm so tired," and he began to cry again. She felt him enter her, plunging up toward the cold nest of milk in her belly. It was going to be too late now to make him stop. She remembered how he had stood at the plate-glass window with his arms spread, his mouth open against the pane. She opened her legs more for him then, trying to feel him before he was gone. He rocked faster, grunted, and collapsed, letting go her wrists. Then he moved off her and slid away, and she stroked his head because she needed to. He scared her, sometimes; that was what she felt.

After a couple of minutes Carl got up and went into the bathroom and she heard his water running into the bowl. She thought of the blank spot on the test, before the answer had come. When Carl came back he fell asleep almost instantly. She watched him sleep. She extended her fingers, touching his throat at the place where the brindle had torn Fred.

In the morning Monica got up early and went to muck out the run. She had forgotten to leave Fred enough food. He was lying in the mud beside the gate, but when he saw her he stood up unsteadily and shook himself. It was a good sign. She fed him, dumping wet and dry food into separate steel mixing bowls. Then she raked the torn-up ground.

In the tall trees behind the house she cleaned off the rake. There were patches of broken ground near the pile of tires. Monica realized that she didn't know exactly where Carl had buried the brindle. She was sweating heavily. It was still early, but so hot. She looked into the scummy water inside the tire rims. It was only water, she thought, you could not see the harm in it; but it was full of harm anyway. You couldn't drink water like that. She wiped sweat off her face.

She was close enough to Troutman's runs to hear his dogs whimpering, though not his radio. Maybe his radio was out, she thought. She felt her ears prickle as she stood listening between the houses. There wasn't even static. Troutman's radio might have been out for hours, but to Monica it seemed as if all those voices had just now disappeared from the face of the earth. What did that mean, "the face of the earth," she thought.

Carl was a man. This thought occurred to her now over and over, in exactly this language. Carl was a man, her husband; Dad was like a man. She felt a spasm of joy deep inside her. Then it came again, sharper. She had to lean against the tires. She could hear Carl's truck start up in their garage. Carl had loved that dog without trying. But it was not like her to be quick that way. This spare life he had put inside her, could she love it more than necessary? Troutman's door banged, and the radio came on and played through the air between the houses. She sank down to the cool earth under the trees. She let go the rake. Her hands were empty. She was going to be happy again in a minute.

A NOTE ON THE TYPE

This book was set in Garamond, a type named for the famous Parisian type cutter Claude Garamond (ca. 1480–1561). Garamond, a pupil of Geoffroy Tory, based his letter on the types of the Aldine Press in Venice, but he introduced a number of important differences, and it is to him that we owe the letter now known as "old style."

Composed by Creative Graphics, Allentown, Pennsylvania
Printed and bound by The Haddon Craftsmen,
an R. R. Donnelley & Sons Company,
Bloomsburg, Pennsylvania
Designed by Robert C. Olsson